Three Blind Wives

Robin H Soprano

Table of Contents

Saying goodbye to people you love hurts.

My two best friends in the whole world are leaving, going separate ways to start new lives. We hug each other tightly, huddling into one another, with tears in our eyes. The Fort Lauderdale airport is busy with other travelers scooting by us. We are in their way but don't care. We don't know when we will see each other again, and our hearts are breaking.

I've known these girls for only seven years, but we all connected right away and have never been apart. I give one last look at Crystal and Dusty, and we make a pact: as soon as they are settled, we will choose a place and meet three times a year on each of our birthdays for a girls' weekend, no matter what.

As I leave the airport, I can't stop the tears running from my eyes. I put on my big, dark sunglasses, head out to the parking area, and get in my car. As I make my way out of the lot, my thoughts are scattered. I still can't believe this is happening.

It all started almost a year ago, during one of our weekly girls' nights at my house. That night, we poured some wine, put out snacks, and Crystal said, "I have a fun idea!"

Five little innocent words that changed our lives forever...

Ten months ago…

"It's gonna be all right, Renee," Dusty says with her perfect, pink smile. "You'll see. I think you and Frank can work this out. He loves you."

"But I don't feel like I love him anymore. Just the sight of him makes me tense."

Crystal picks up the bottle of merlot, tops off our glasses, and sighs dramatically. "Okay, I'll say it, Renee. I think you are having postpartum depression. You have knocked out two babies in a year and a half. I think you should ask the doctor for some drugs."

"What? No, I'm fine," I inform my friends. "The separation is good for me, right now. It's only been a few weeks, and I already feel less tension." I notice they both give each other a look.

"Okay. Fine." Dusty sighs. "Just don't do anything extreme for a while."

"Agreed!" Crystal raises her wine glass. "Dusty and I are divorced and have good reasons," she spits out. "Our husbands were cheats, liars, and pricks. Not Frank—you got a good one there. If you need time, take it. But I'm telling you, he truly loves you, and this is killing him."

"Can we please talk about something else?" I urge, feeling my temper rise.

"Fine," Crystal huffs. "Listen, I have a fun idea. Now, hear me out. It's just for shits and giggles. There is this online dating service called *Blind Date*. I say we get on it and go on some dates, see what's out there."

Dusty looks up from her wine glass, eyes wide behind her big, horn-rimmed glasses, and laughs. "There's nothing out there, and all the guys in our age group want girls in their twenties."

"Oh, I don't know," I answer. "I wouldn't mind sticking my toes in the water, just for fun." Raising my hand, I add, "I'm not looking for anything serious."

"Yep—me, too," Crystal agrees with me. "We are older, wiser; we know what we want and how we want it. We are independently wealthy, and we can take this opportunity into our own hands. Our rules. Let them buy us drinks and dinner, and then WE decide if we are going to fuck 'em and dump 'em!"

"So, kind of like we are the guys?" Dusty asks.

We all look at each other, nodding our perfectly hairstyled heads.

"Where're your contacts?" Crystal asks Dusty.

"Don't worry—I won't wear my glasses on a date. I hate them. I only need them, you know, to see..." Dusty's tone is sarcastic.

"Good. Now, let me show you the website." Crystal jumps up from my couch and heads to the office, where the computer is. A few clicks later we are reading: *WELCOME TO BLIND DATE.*

"This is what I propose we do. We set up one profile for the three of us. It does not require a picture, hence the whole blind-date theme. Although it says you can choose to send photos once you exchange cell numbers or make a date. Let's see...Make up a name."

We all quickly lose any train of thought as we first spew out the obvious stripper names.

"Candie?"

"NO!"

"Ginger?"

"NO!"

"Brittney?"

"NO! Come on," I say. "We are in our forties. These guys are going to think we're in our twenties with those names."

Crystal points a French-painted nail at the screen. "Right here it says age group twenty-five to thirty-five, thirty-five to forty-five, and then, fifty and up. Really?" she huffs. "I'm forty-eight, and I look pretty fabulous. What would I want with a sixty-five-year-old? All I see is old balls coming at me!" She shakes her head and makes a vomit sound. "I'm NOT that old yet!"

"Let's lie a little," Dusty offers. "We can fake it. Renee is the youngest of all of us—she's forty-one—so put thirty-five to forty-five. I think it's reasonable. And I also think we'd better hit some yoga and exercise classes at my spa. We may need to just tone it up a little. I don't know about you girls, but if a man is going to see me naked, I want to make sure everything stays in place."

I look at Dusty and Crystal. Yes, they are older than I am, but both are beautiful. "Not fair. You both have been nipped and tucked. I just do a little Botox here and there, and I've had two babies."

Dusty looks up from the computer and pushes her glasses up her nose. "True, Crystal and I let my ex tweak us up before I divorced him, but you're still young, Renee.

A few rounds in the gym and you'll be fine. You've lost all your baby weight. Now just tone up a little. Plus, the exercise will be good for the stamina. We're gonna need it for the younger guys!"

"What was it like being married to a plastic surgeon?" I ask Dusty. "I would feel like he was constantly looking at my imperfections."

"Not Kenny. He was too busy fucking all the franken-barbies he created in his operating room."

"I'm just glad I got my tits done before you hired me to clean his clock," Crystal says with a laugh. "The best part was that he actually hit on me, too. And you should have seen his face months later when I entered the courtroom as Dusty's divorce attorney. There I am with my new boobs, proving infidelity! He knew he was beat."

We all laugh at that. "I love some of these stories you two talk about. I wish I'd known you guys back then," I say.

"You found us at just the right time." Dusty smiles. "It's when we started to live and have fun."

"I'll drink to that," Crystal chimes in as she raises her wine glass. "I was a nasty bitch when I was married to Greg. The thing that bothered me the most was finding out he married me for my money. The cheating was another thing, because half the time he was drunk, and I was told he couldn't get it up most of the time. No, it was the gambling, and lying, and losing my money. I don't think Greg Walker worked over a month at any job in his life."

I stare at Crystal like she's someone I don't recognize. "I just don't see how someone like you ended up with such a loser like him."

"He was different. And younger. Lots of fun. I didn't get married till I was thirty-seven. I think I was scared. I worked my life away. Now I'm alone again. No kids. My mother, the merry widow, is having more fun than I am, especially since she sold the house in Canada and moved to the south of France. I can't wait to go see her."

"Your mom is my idol," Dusty coos. "But I'm happy I have the spa and rehab center. It keeps me busy, and I have a wonderful staff. It's nice to provide a private, elegant, comfortable place for ladies recovering from plastic or reconstructive surgeries, too."

"Okay, girls," Crystal cuts in. "Back to the profile. Thirty-five to forty-five. Check."

"How about the name Anna?" I ask. "It's simple, short, sweet."

The girls look at me and nod in agreement. We put *average* curvy body type and fill in *yes* on the *job* line but don't mention what kind. *Yes,* to a car. *Yes,* to pets, since Dusty has a ranch with horses. We also put down *just dating, nothing serious* about relationship goals.

Finally, we hit *Enter*, and within a few minutes we are up on *Blind Date*. We start to maneuver around and read men's profiles. Some are funny, some are very dirty, and then we see a few normal ones. Crystal is the first to go and text one of them a *Hey there—want to chat?* And soon we all join in and find profiles of men we think would be fun to chat and maybe set up a date with. We synchronize the website with our individual emails, so when someone responds, we'll know.

About three days later, we are flooded with responses. As usual, Crystal is the first to chat with a guy—named Brad—and sets up a date on a Thursday night. She tells us where it will be and says she will text us if she gets in any trouble so we can swoop in for a rescue. The night following the date, we will meet at Dusty's ranch for girls' night to hear all about Crystal's evening with Brad.

***

Friday night, as planned, we all gather at the ranch. Sprawling acreage. Four beautiful horses in a magnificent stable. All Colorado-style brown wood and stone. Dusty had even named the ranch Crooked Pines due to the few pine trees that grew there in a twisted and curved shape. I pull down her long driveway and park my Mercedes next to Crystal's BMW. Before I get to the big front door, Dusty opens it and lets me in.

We sit in front of her cave-like fireplace and nestle into her soft, smooth, brown-leather sofas, our toes enjoying the texture of animal-skin throw rugs tossed about the floor. The place is warm and cozy except for the few deer heads mounted on the walls. Dusty loves to hunt. Me? I would turn vegetarian before I shot and killed an animal for food; it's just not in me. I eat meat, but I pretend I don't know where it comes from.

Dusty pulls a cork from a bottle of merlot and pours generously into three wine goblets. Crystal has a smug look on her face.

"Wait till you girls hear this."

Once we are all settled in again with our wine, Crystal raises her eyebrows and begins. "Well, the date with Brad was interesting. He said he is an entrepreneur, in what business he wasn't clear. He said he has his hands in a little bit of everything. To me, that means he's broke or out of work and a bullshitter, but he is very handsome—very tan and fit—and he knows it. I think that's how he gets by. He said he's forty-five. I met him at the Polo Club, and we had drinks first then decided to have dinner. He's fun and sexy, and that's the only reason I stayed. He thinks my name is Anna, of course.

"After dinner, he walked me to my car and literally grabbed me. Put his hand right up my shirt, went for the tits instantly. I was shocked at first, but the kiss was so hot! I just softened into him, took his bait, and rode it. I pressed myself right up against him, and I could feel him get hard. Ladies, he has one hell of a package under his jeans, and I think I'll see him again, so I can get a look at it!"

We giggle and sip our wine. "Did you make another date already?" I ask with enthusiasm.

"Oh yes," Crystal replies with a devilish smile. "We are meeting again tomorrow night at the Blue Moon for dinner and then…" She rolls her eyes for dramatic flair.

"So, you're going to sleep with Brad," says Dusty.

"I'm not saying yes or no, I'm just saying it is very possible."

"Go for it," I offer enthusiastically. "I've got someone online, too. He wants to meet me. I'm thinking about it."

The girls look at me, their eyes wide with delight. "Really?! Let's read his profile," Dusty says, grabbing the laptop. A few clicks and we're on.

Crystal points at the little envelope icon. "Hey, the mailbox is full."

"Click on it. See what these guys have to say," I remark with a little sarcasm.

Dusty taps the first one. "This dude is using the name STAR69. I can only imagine."

Hey Anna, I want to lick your pussy all night. How about a taste?

"Holy shit!" I spit out. "How rude can you get?"

"Okay. And...he's deleted," Dusty says.

"Well, what did you expect? He's using the name STAR69. Come on!"

"Next up?" Dusty reads, "BIG DADDY," and clicks on the message.

Howdy, Anna. I read your profile. You sound like a fun filly. Come read my profile. Maybe you'll like it, too. Sure would be nice to take you out.

We check out BIG DADDY's profile to find he's from Texas, lives near here now, is retired, and is about sixty-five years old. Crystal reaches over Dusty's shoulder and hits delete. "No old balls!" she snaps.

"Next," I say with a laugh.

Hi, Anna, you sound sweet. My name is Carlo. Please feel free to check out my profile. Chat with me—see if we click.

Dusty hits the chat button. Carlo is online.

Hi there, we type.

Hello, how are you? Is this Anna?

Fine. Yes.

Did you read my profile? What do you think?

Quickly, we search his profile. Carlo, forty-six, single father of three. Lives in the area. Italian and Spanish descent, born here in the States. Looking for love and a relationship. "Yeah, they all say that," Crystal snarls.

Hi. Yes, read your profile. Would very much like to meet you.

"I'd like to meet him," Dusty says.

Back and forth they text, setting up a time to chat again and to discuss a place for a date. Then we click over to the guy I am interested in.

"He says his name is Steve. Here it is." I quickly point out his profile.

Dusty reads aloud: "Steve, forty-eight years old. Single, never married, owns his own business, truck driver, originally from Philly, lives and works in the area. Wants to date a nice woman—nothing serious. Okay," she continues. "Let's see if he's online."

"Doesn't look like he's on at the moment, but let's leave him a message," I offer. "I was chatting with him a little bit last night. I'm not picking up any creep factor, but you never know."

Hello, Steve. If you would like to go on a date, message me soon and we will make plans. Anna.

***

Saturday morning, we all meet at Dusty's spa, Raging Beauty.

We do a Zumba class then stretch with some yoga, take a swim, and have relaxing massages. One of the attendants brings us some frozen cocktails, and we sit in lounge chairs by the pool.

"I heard from Steve," I say. "We are going to meet at that sports pub on main and first—T.K.O.'s—Thursday night."

"Good for you, Renee. Now remember," Crystal says as she looks at me with her icy blue eyes, "you're only separated, so don't do anything crazy you might regret. You should just date. Don't go jumping into bed yet."

"I agree." Dusty lifts her frozen glass.

I take a deep breath and slowly let it out. "Thanks for your concern, girls, but I wasn't planning on crazy, just fun. See what happens."

"Trust me," Crystal replies. "Your wounds are fresh, and you're vulnerable. Play it safe or else you will just get more confused and hurt. I still wish you would go see your doctor or a therapist."

"I'm fine. Seriously, let me breathe."

"She's right," Dusty counters. "Nothing wrong with a little breather. Just remember that's all it is. Maybe dating some strange men will make you realize if you want to stay married or not."

Crystal finishes her drink with a slurp on her straw. "Okay, Friday night, my house, and we tell each other about our dates. Do you want red or white wine?"

I toss her a look of derision. "Both." I snort a laugh.

CHAPTER 2

Renee Nobel.

It's been a hell of a week. Frank came by twice to see the babies. He wanted a hug, but I just couldn't do it. I just feel nothing, and all I can think about is my date with Steve. I pull out three different outfits and decide on skinny jeans paired with a deep-neckline shirt—good for a sports pub, I figure. Sensual, middle-of-the-road sexy, not too revealing, but something Grandma wouldn't wear, either.

I leave my house at seven sharp and get to T.K.O.'s in fifteen minutes. Two champion fighters own the bar, but I have no idea who they are, and it's not a shabby place for being a low-key hangout. I get a text that Steve is on his way in. I reply, Me too, and shuffle through the entrance.

* * *

Dusty Bruno.

I recently placed an ad for a ranch hand in the local newspaper after I'd had to let yet another one go due to the fact they'd lied about actually knowing how to handle horses. This time, the ad had only been in the paper four days when a call came in.

"Hi, is this Miss Bruno? My name is Gage Destry. I'm calling about the ranch-hand job in the paper. Is this the Crooked Pine Ranch?"

"Yes, it is," I answer then continue a little too enthusiastically, "Please, Gage, tell me you have equine experience. It is my biggest problem here. They always say they do, but I end up with a disaster."

"Yes, Ma'am, I have a lot of experience. I grew up on my family's ranch in Montana."

"Great," I answer. "When can you come out for an interview?"

"I'm right up the road if now's a good time."

I am caught off guard a little bit, but there is something in his voice that seems decent or real. And I think, Why not?

"Sure, Gage, come on down."

It only takes about five minutes until a black Chevy Silverado dually pulls in my driveway. The truck looks a little old and beat-on, but sturdy all the same. I watch from the window as this strong-looking man approaches the front door. Jeans, boots, T-shirt, a wheat-colored cowboy hat tipped low on his brow, and sunglasses. I answer the door and instantly note this is not a boy—oh no. This is a six-foot, well-muscled man who takes his hat off in my presence.

"Ma'am," he says in a husky voice. I let him in.

"Please have a seat, and you may call me Dusty."

* * *

Renee.

As I walk through the doorway into the bar, I feel a tap on my shoulder.

"Anna?"

I whirl on my heel to study a pair of blue eyes and a very nice smile. "Yes," I answer and smile back.

"Hi! I figured it was you because you said on the phone you had long, red hair."

He is adorable, and all I can do is nod at him.

He laughs and opens the next set of doors.

17

"Shall we?"

We find a nice, quiet booth and sit across from each other.

"You smell nice."

My "thank you" comes out garbled and broken. I self-consciously clear my throat and continue, "I'm sorry; I'm very nervous."

He reaches for my hand, and I accommodate. "Nothing to be nervous about," he says. "Have you done the online thing before?"

I swallow hard. "No, this is new to me." *Why am I so nervous? My heart is pounding ridiculously hard!*

"Okay," he declares, "let's get some drinks and relax."

Can he see I'm a bundle of nerves? I've got to pull myself together.

I manage to tell the server I would like a chardonnay. Then I take a deep breath. "How about you? You do online dating a lot?"

He nods his head, looking a little embarrassed about his answer. "Yes, unfortunately it's not my first picnic."

"Are you divorced?" I ask.

"No, I've never been married."

How weird—he's forty-eight and never been married? This could be a red flag. But then again, I'm not looking for anything serious, right? I'm here to have fun.

"Have you ever been in a serious relationship?" I question.

"Yes, it lasted ten years. We were engaged, and then she cheated on me."

That sucks. But ten years? Shit or get off the pot. I would have cheated, too.

"Oh, I'm sorry [*not really*]. How long ago was this?"

"Over twelve years ago. Then I moved down here to Fort Lauderdale. Fresh start."

"You've been here about twelve years, and you haven't found anyone?"

"Sadly, no. But I am having fun."

***

Dusty.

"So, tell me, Gage, what kind of experience do you have?"

He is obviously not shy. He strides up right in front of me, only a few feet from my body. He smells like leather and aftershave, even though he has the sexiest scruff on his dimple-cheeked face and around that sharp jaw.

"Well, like I said on the phone, I grew up on a horse and cattle ranch in Montana. My father and granddaddy and my great-granddaddy all were cattle men. We broke a lot of horses over the years, and some people would bring us horses that no one else could handle, but we made 'em into good-broke horses. Never met a horse I didn't like, especially a mare. I suppose you could say us Destry men have a way with females."

I shrug. "Do you? Well, we'll see about that. I have two mares and two geldings in the stable out back. Let me introduce you."

He holds out his arm and gestures with his well-worn cowboy hat. "Lead the way."

We get to the stable, and he immediately knows how to talk to and handle my horses; his voice is soft, his touch is gentle, and I can sense his years of experience along with an innate ability. I am awestruck.

"So, you're like a horse whisperer?"

He smiles, white teeth flashing before me as his dimples get deeper set. What a sight.

"Yeah, I guess it's something like that. A hundred years ago, the Native Americans helped my great-granddaddy cultivate the land, and I suppose you could say they taught us a great deal about our animals and the respect they need to get them to trust and respect you back."

I commented, "Well, that sounds exactly like my own philosophy. But with the knowledge it seems like you have, are you sure you will be satisfied cleaning stalls, fixing fence, and only working with a few horses on a small stable like this? You don't want to work at one of the bigger facilities?"

"Ma'am, I'd much rather work at a smaller place and feel like I'm really needed, where I can give my attention to a few good horses instead of a barnful that are just dollar signs to some big trainer. I can see your horses are in good shape, and you've got a real nice place, but I'll bet it's hard to keep it up all by yourself...uh...if you are by yourself, that is."

"Yes, I am. And since I have a business to run, too, it is tough to get everything done around here and work with the horses as much as they need."

"I'd sure be glad to help you out with that."

I just stand there, staring at him. *Is he for real?*

I put out my hand to shake his. "Gage, you've got the job. When can you start?"

He looks around, gives me a once-over from top to bottom and back. "Right now. My stuff's in the truck. The ad said something about an apartment above the garage. Is it ready to be occupied?"

I nod. "But first, follow me. I'll show you the main house. The apartment doesn't have much of a kitchen, so you can basically consider mine part of a common area. Then you can grab your stuff and we'll head to the apartment next." I stop and look over my shoulder at him before adding, "Welcome to Crooked Pines, Gage."

* * *

Crystal Monrie.

"Hi, Mom. How are you? How's the French Riviera?"

"Oh, it's beautiful. You must come soon, oui? I have a beautiful cottage. I stroll the beach every day, sit in the garden at night with Gaetan—ahhh...he is loving me. I am so very happy."

"I'm glad, Mom. I hope to come see you soon. Work is hectic right now, but I'll plan something."

"Crystal, too much work and no play...how will you find love, mon ange? I worry. You need to be loved by a man, by a good man. I find you one, *oui*?"

I laugh. "Mom, if I can't find a good one, how will you? Please don't worry about me. I'm fine, honestly. What am I going to do with you?"

"Ahh, I am your mother, *mon coeur*. I know how to find you a good man."

"Okay, Mom. I gotta go. Good luck with that. Let me know how it works out. Bye, Mama."

"*Au revoir, mon ange.* Have some fun!"

My sweet mother—her life is all put together. Maybe I should entertain the idea of her finding me a man. I shake my head and giggle at the thought.

I wonder how Renee's date is going?

***

Renee.

Our food comes, and I start to feel the effects of two glasses of chardonnay. I am beginning to get the feeling Steve is a player. His phone rings too much, and my gut thinks its other ladies, but I feel okay with it. After all, technically I am still married, so I don't want anything serious.

As we eat, my thoughts run wild. *Dear God, what a cutie!* Dark-blue eyes, just a light touch of grey in his tousled hair, and a very trim goatee. He isn't very tall—maybe an inch taller than I am, around five-nine or -ten. The big, well-toned muscles in his arms are displaying some ink.

He is talking about his time in the navy and how he loves riding his Harley. This could be just the fun I am looking for. After a while of sitting with empty plates and awkward silence, I lean over the table and ask him if he wants to kiss me.

He gives me a crooked smile and replies, "Yes, I do."

So, I lean in a little more, but he doesn't budge. I give him a questioning eyebrow.

"Oh...not in here. Let's go outside," he whispers.

He pays the bill and walks me to my car. Before I know it, his arms are around my waist and our lips smash together. Then his tongue invades my mouth, and he turns me so my back is up against my car and his body presses against mine. Just as Crystal's date had done, Steve goes right for the boobs.

Maybe there's a men's handbook somewhere, I think.

We kiss long and hard, as if it is keeping us alive. My heart pounds in my ears. I'm getting aroused. But before I can say "Stop!" he says it for me.

"I think you'd better get in your car and get home, little girl. Too much too fast. We need to spread it out and take it slow."

"Okay. Fine with me," I answer, out of breath.

He opens my car door and helps me in, gazing at me as if I'm candy, and kisses me once more with deep seduction.

Yes, this dude is a player. He must have read somewhere how to please a woman. I bet he's hot in bed.

That thought alone had me squeezing my legs together.

We exchange cell numbers before he says softly, "Good night, Anna. Sweet dreams."

I watch him swagger away. I don't know where he parked or what kind of vehicle he has. The parking lot is full, and by the time I back out, he's gone.

About an hour after I'm home, while getting ready for bed, I hear a text come through on my cell.

Had fun. Are you all warm and fuzzy?
I laugh and think, *Yeah, player. Big time.*
I text back but keep it short:
Yes.

CHAPTER 3

Dusty.

I wake up early, remembering I have a new stable hand on the premises. I check the time: 5:45 a.m. I pad barefoot into my kitchen to start the coffee. But on the way, I notice the telltale aroma already wafting through my house, and there he is—Gage, wide awake and drinking from one of my mugs.

"Good morning, sleepyhead. You always sleep so late?"

He slowly walks up to me and places a mug of coffee in my hands. "I already fed and watered the horses, cleaned the stalls. Gotta run into town next. Looks like you're low on feed. If you're okay with changing their feed, I think a higher-protein formula might be better for them as we get them workin' more. Then I'll start on the two mares, today. Just do some ground work, groom 'em real good, get 'em to trust me a little."

I silently stand, a little in disbelief. "You did all...What time did you get up?"

He smiles. "Earlier than you."

"Okay, sure. I guess you've got this."

He puts his hat back on. As he makes his way out the door, he turns back. "This is nothing, by the way. Back home, I had cattle to rustle up, too. And I'm gonna start a list of repairs you need tended to. I'll get on that later this afternoon."

He tips his head and swooshes out the door. I'm still frozen to the ground as I watch him go about his work. He is a fine specimen. And he still smells good!

* * *

Renee.

All I can think about is that player, Steve, as I sit here and feed the baby. I know I shouldn't even care, but it was fun to have someone kiss and manhandle me a little bit. It felt good, and I want more of that. My husband used to be like that. What happens to that passion? Why doesn't it last?

I'm just finishing cleaning up when a text chimes. It's from Steve:

Good morning. Can I see you Friday night?

Reading that makes my heart jump, but it also makes me a little nauseous. Even though it feels fun, it also feels wrong. I text him back a *yes*, and he proceeds with,

Hope you have a great day.

I just leave it at that for now. I feel a little confused. I almost want to call my husband, Frank, and ask him for advice. Ha! Wouldn't that be hilarious?

I turn on the T.V. and put the baby down for her nap. The background noise is soothing for us both, but I just wish the news wasn't so depressing as sadly the anchor declares there's been another victim attacked by the crazy rapist running around. To distract myself, I decide to go check the *Blind Date* site. *That should be good for some laughs.*

Opening the app, I notice the messages are full. "Okay, guys—show me what ya got."

* * *

Crystal.

Almost lunch, thank God. I need the break.

I reach for my cell and call Renee.

"Hey. What's going on?" she says.

"Uh…I need a lunch break."

Renee chuckles. "YOU? You never take a lunch break unless some big-shot attorney is buying."

"Yes, you know me so well. It's been crazy this morning. I need a diversion. Hey—how'd the date go last night?"

"It went really well. I like him...a lot...and I shouldn't."

"You'd better watch yourself, you little slut. You're gonna get in trouble," I tell her, laughing. "What happened? Is he hot? Built?"

"Oh...God, Crystal. We kissed. I got wet...my crotch got wet. I can't remember the last time that happened. I was beginning to think my vajayjay might be broken."

I snort with a laugh. "Did you check your batteries?"

"Batteries? Oh, you're not funny. But if I go on another date with him, I might need to buy something because—yep—I'm gonna need release!"

"So, what else is going on?"

"I'm on the *Blind Date* site, our in-box is full, and there sure are some whack-a-doos on here. Holy shit! Do men not have a filter? What makes them think typing dirty sex talk or showing pictures of their junk is going to make any of us hit the yes button for a date?"

I scramble with my mouse. "Oh, let me check, too. I'm clicking on. Let's see what we've got here."

"Hey, Crystal, this one sounds good for you: GOLDMAGNUM73. He sounds just the right age and size! Look at that thing—that's gotta be Photoshopped."

I laugh. "Yeah, with that code name, he's probably short and has a little dick." I search through some more names, "Oh, I like the sound of this one. 'THE GRADUATE, looking for my Mrs. Robinson.'"

"I saw that one, too." Renee laughs. "What do you think?"

"I think I'm going to send him a hello. It says he is twenty-five and likes a mature woman. Hmm...might have a mommy complex, but that's okay. I haven't had a twenty-something in a long time."

"Go for it!" Renee squeals. "See if he takes the bait."

I read aloud for Renee as I type:

Hello, Graduate. I may be what you're looking for.

Hello, could you be my Mrs. Robinson? THE GRADUATE responds.

I could. Want to find out? I flirt back.

I hear Renee laughing over the phone before he continues:

Sure, let's meet. Are you free Friday night?

I am. Tell me where and what time. I'll be there.

OK, sweetness, 7pm at the Bar Nova on Derbyshire Blvd. You know it?

I do. See you then, I answer.

"My God, Crystal. He just sounds like a one-night stand to me."

"Hmm. Maybe," I say. "But remember, it's for fun and it's on our own terms."

* * *

Dusty.

Since Gage has everything under control at my ranch, I decide to pop in at my spa and make like a boss. It's a busy day, and we just admitted two women recovering from plastic surgery.

One lady is in her late sixties—went for a full facelift. She's sedated but in pain. I told her it will be worth all the misery overall.

The other client is a young girl who has been modeling, and this is her second surgery. First it was her nose and chin; now it's a boob job. I didn't see anything wrong with her in the first place and she's only in her twenties. What these agencies do to these young girls! She might need therapy someday.

I make my way to my office after an inventory check and think, *Let me see what's going on in Blind Date.*

I notice either Crystal or Renee made a date of some sort with THE GRADUATE. Then I see a message from Carlos.

Can't wait to hear from you. Looking forward to a date!

I smile. *He sounds normal enough,* I reason as I send him a reply:

Me too!

Short, sweet, to the point. That's me. I shoot a text to both my friends, asking who made a date with THE GRADUATE. Crystal responds with *"That would be me."* And I learn Renee has another date, too.

I send out another text suggesting that because the two of them have dates on Friday, we should have girls' night Saturday at my house to catch up.

The answer is a unanimous *yes.*

I fall into my big leather chair. It groans along with me as I relax and sit deeper. The soft leather hugs my body, and the smell of it automatically reminds me of Gage. I wonder how he's doing.

***

Renee.

"I said no, Frank. Please don't push. I need space and time. The more you smother me, the more I'll move further away from you."

Frank looks at me, and my heart breaks, but I can't help the way I feel. I just don't want him around me.

"Please, baby. I love you. I believe you need to see the doctor. I truly think you have postpartum depression. Why can't you just go and humor me? Go ahead and prove me wrong, if nothing else."

"I'm fine!" I yell back. "Why can't you just let me be for a while and see where this goes? Maybe I'm just not in love with you any more, Frank. I'm sorry it hurts you to hear that, but it's how I feel at this moment. I think you've had enough time with the girls today. Could you just go now? Please!"

He stares at me for what seems like an hour. It's almost frightening.

"Fine. Sure. I don't want to make you angry. I'll never be far from you and the girls—do you understand? Just in case you need me for anything...at any time."

I nod as he hugs Dawn and Mandy. Soon after he leaves, I cry. I cry hard.

* * *

Dusty.

I'm feeling tired as I pull into my driveway. I was up early but not as early as Gage. I still don't know what inhumane time that man got up. I didn't even hear him come into the main house and make coffee.

Once inside, I just want to get out of my clothes and into a big shirt and yoga pants. Putting my hair in a twist and securing it with a clip, I walk to the back windows that overlook the yard and stable. There's Gage, up on a ladder, hammering above the barn doors. I've known they were loose but hadn't gotten around to fixing them yet. Gage is shirtless, wearing just his jeans and hat. He has quite the physique. He notices me and waves.

35

A few minutes later, Gage makes his way into the house. That swagger of his makes me smile.

"Good afternoon, Ma'am," he says as he takes off his hat. There's just a hint of sweat on him, and his leather-and-aftershave scent reaches me, filling me like a cool forest breeze.

"I fixed those barn doors and got some higher-protein feed but not the brand I really like. Your feed store here is limited, so I might check online for it, but let's see how they do first with this."

"Thank you, Gage. You went beyond what was expected, and I appreciate that."

"I worked with the two mares a while today. Just doing some groundwork and getting to know them a little. They're good horses, and I can make them even better."

"Really?" This shocks me; my geldings are pretty quiet, but my mares are a little witchy. "I'd love to watch you work with the others."

We go out to the barn, and Gage brings each horse out of its stall to lead them out to their respective paddocks. One by one, the beautiful animals walk past me, and I give them a pat on the neck. Jeremial was first, then Chamuel, Miguel, and the youngest, Ariel.

"This is mommy's girl," I say to Gage, as she turns to not-so-gently nudge me with her head, almost pushing me off my feet. I laugh but admit, "She does this to me all the time. This is the kind of bad habit I'm not the best at correcting."

Gage watches her for a moment. "Seems to me she's trying to tell you something. You gotta let them know what they're not allowed to do. Just like with a kid. Can't let them just get away with whatever they want. But you gotta let them know when they do something right, too. They'll respect you for it in the end.

"That's really true! They all tell me things in their own ways. I got each one of them as a gift to myself. Every time I thought I was defeated, or something tried to destroy me and didn't, I bought a horse. My way of knowing I'm strong, just like them."

Gage nods. "Yes, now it makes more sense with their names. You gave them names of the Archangels."

I smile up at him. "You got that?" I squint and wrinkle my nose.

"Yes, Ma'am. I don't live under a rock."

"I think I'm impressed you know that."

"Well then, let's see." He starts with Ariel. "Archangel Ariel helps us provide for our physical needs. Next, we have Chamuel, who eases anxiety, brings a personal pace and peace. Then we have Jeremial—this guy helps to heal emotional wounds and helps plan positive change. Finally, Miguel, or Michael, the most popular Archangel. Now, he's one of the toughest angels. He releases us from fear and doubt, two of the worst things we can do to ourselves. I can't imagine as fine a woman as yourself having any of those issues."

Gage's voice is soft and warm, his eyes kind, his hands strong and sure as he tenderly strokes Ariel before turning her loose to run, kick, and play for a few moments before dropping her head to graze.

"Well, like I said, they helped me with those issues."

After cleaning their stalls, Gage takes Miguel, the youngest of the two geldings, out of the paddock and brings him to the barn, talking to him and moving quietly and surely around him while he snaps Miguel to the cross-ties. Gage deftly goes through the process of currying, brushing, and finally running a soft towel over the shiny coat to make it shine even more. He then picks up each hoof and cleans it out with the hoof pick, checking to see there is no disease or abnormality that needs treatment.

Next, out in the riding arena, Gage does some groundwork with Miguel, getting the horse to lead quietly beside him as Gage walks forward, moves him backward, and does some slow turns. He seems pleased that Miguel knows what "whoa" means. Tying Miguel at the fence, Gage takes the saddle and bridle from their rack and begins to tack him up. He then climbs confidently into the saddle and moves the horse in big circles, tighter circles, and figure-eights, working on flexibility and collection, I realize.

Gage seems to communicate so subtly with the animal. I can barely see his hands or legs move as he gives the cues. Miguel, in turn, flows through his gaits and turns more smoothly than I have ever seen him. He looks calm and at ease, like he already trusts Gage will do the right thing with him.

I think I know how he feels. I don't know how this man came to be here, but I want to know more about him.

"Okay, now I'm really impressed. Wow, he is really taking a liking to you. I can't wait to see you work with the mares."

"It's really all just perseverance and patience. Being calm and confident with them. They're herd animals, so they look at their rider or handler as a leader. If you give off a sense that everything is safe and okay, they pick up on that."

"Hey, Gage—you have plans for dinner?" I ask boldly and surprise myself.

"No, I do not. Whatcha got in mind?"

"How about some barbecue up at the house? We can have dinner on the patio. Say, around seven?"

"Sounds good, Dusty. Thanks! I'll finish up the rest of the chores and put some hay in to the horses. See you later."

As I walk back towards the house, I can feel his eyes on me, but I don't turn to look back.

CHAPTER 4

Crystal.

"I'll have a dry martini, please," I tell the bartender at Bar Nova. He has the drink in front of me in a matter of seconds. When I came in a few minutes ago, I found a seat at the bar that strategically put me in line with the door, and I made sure I was here early to maybe see which guy Mr. Graduate is when he walks in.

I slowly savor my three-olive martini—I told him earlier that's what I would be drinking. Finally, after a while, the door glides open and in walks this young, handsome twenty-something, a little too Brad Pitt-looking for my taste, but it could be worse. He spots me, and I raise my glass. His smile is big and bright—a good sign.

"Hello...Anna?" he asks cautiously.

"Hello, yourself," I quip. "So, you got a name, handsome?"

"Jason. Jason Morgan. Pleasure to meet you."

I give him a once-over, up and down. He looks normal enough. "How old are you, Jason?"

"Twenty-five; I hope this isn't a problem for you, Anna."

"No, not a problem. I'm just afraid I might break you, is all," I say with a crooked smile.

His responding laugh is cute, his teeth a brilliant white and straight. He looks like money. He looks like his parents' money.

"May I buy you dinner, my lady?" he asks, bowing with humor. I like him.

"Yes, you may." I take his arm as we proceed out of the bar to the restaurant's dining room. They seat us in a nice, quiet booth in the back. As we pick up our menus, I notice the waiter is already bringing Jason a drink, "Jack and Coke, sir."

"You must come here often; they seem to know you well."

"Yes, I started to come here after I landed my job at the firm, relocated after college.

"The firm?" I ask. "Are you a lawyer?"

"No, advertising firm."

"Oh, I'm a divorce attorney. That's why I asked."

"Wow! Divorce attorney. Sadly, you must be busy."

"Yes," I answer, "as a matter of fact, I am."

"It's a shame," he continues. "No one puts any effort into relationships like they used to. My parents have been married forever."

I smile at him. "Well, unfortunately, there are a lot of asshole people out there, and not just men. Some women marry only for money, and eventually the guy realizes he's made a terrible mistake."

The waiter comes back, and we order. Our conversation through dinner is quite enjoyable. The kid is well educated and articulate. And I was right: he comes from money. That's not a bad thing, though. I do, too, so I can spot our commonalities. Also, he is delightfully flirtatious. Truly adorable.

"Jason, don't you want to know my age?" I ask, playing with him a bit.

"Nope, it does not matter to me. I have a thing for mature women."

"Okay, then what would you like to do next?"

He reaches for my hand and softly, gently holds it. "Well, my dear, I'd like to take you on a stroll along the beach, maybe pick up a bottle of wine, and take you to my place, or yours."

Is he for real? I think...then think again...

"Okay. Sounds good. Your place."

***

Renee.

"I HAVE NOTHING TO WEAR!" I shout into my closet. I just have all these mommy clothes. Everything I own screams, "Look at me—I'm a mother of two kids and I'm forty!" I drop down on my closet floor, almost in tears. I call my sister up in New Jersey.

"Hello, Renee. You okay?"

"Umm...no. I have a date in an hour, and I have no clothes. I'm seriously going to hyperventilate."

"Okay, calm down. First of all, you do have clothes. Women would kill for your closet. Second, why do you have a date? You should not date until your hormones get back to normal."

"Lisa, I don't need a mom right now; I need help."

"That's exactly what I'm talking about. If you were in your right mind, this would not be a problem for you. You're conflicted."

"Can we not do this? And just help me, please!"

"Fine. Black."

"What?"

"Black."

"Black? Why do you keep saying black?"

"I'm helping you. Wear black, all black. Black is slimming, it's cool and hot at the same time, and it goes with everything and any situation. Dressed up...or just hanging around. Where are you going on this date?"

"Dinner and a movie," I answer like I'm a contestant on a game show.

"Good. Not formal, easygoing. Think dark jeans or black ones, black top or a top with black in it, black sandals..."

"I have it! Yes. Okay...but...grrrr," I grumble.

"What is it?"

"They look completely worn out and old. I'm going to have some shopping to do."

"Renee, you're going to a movie and dinner. I'm sure it's nothing fancy. So put your friggin' jeans on and stop this nonsense. This is all really because, I think, deep down, you don't want to go. I'm guessing most of the clothes are the ones Frank bought you, or that you bought and wore with him. Look, sister, I love you with all my heart and nobody knows you like I do. Here's the deal, sunshine: if you really wanted a divorce, you would have been to a lawyer already. If you were ready to date, you wouldn't be on the phone with me, freaking out over something like clothes. And I'm guessing you're about to cry right now."

Tears stream down my face. Somehow, she makes sense, but I'm not sure what I'm crying about. "I hate you," I say endearingly into my phone as she laughs at me.

"It's gonna be all right, Renee. It's just...whatever you are doing down in Florida, please take it slow, and for Christ's sake, be careful. There's some scumbag running around, raping women, killing them with a sledgehammer. It's been all over the news, even up here. Where is Frank, by the way?"

"He's actually close by. I see him a few times a week because of the girls, but I wish he wouldn't come around that much. Maybe I need to miss him. I don't know, but I am so confused."

"Frank loves you. Just remember that. And whatever it is you're going through, I know it's going to lift one day, so don't do anything you'll regret."

I end the call, go splash cold water on my face, and try to pull it together and get ready for this date. My nanny, Maria, comes in to clean, and she looks at me while shaking her head and whispering to herself under her breath in Spanish.

"Oh, not you, too!" I shout.

***

Dusty.

I pour myself a glass of wine, and Gage opens a Coors, his beer of choice. He takes the two raw steaks I have in my hands and smiles as he tosses them onto the grill.

"I'll cook 'em up for us. Have a seat and enjoy that wine."

I lift my glass to him. "Thanks! Best idea I've heard all week."

As he cooks, I hungrily take in every move his ass and legs make in his snug-fitting

Wranglers and I can see his muscular back and arms flex with even the smallest actions.

"So, Dusty, what does one do around here for fun? I'd only been here a short time when I happened to see the job here in the local *Penny Saver*." He glances in my direction with a smirk.

"We have the usual clubs, sports bars, and pubs. I think there are some rodeos and other horse events you might like over in Davie, which isn't too far away. There are some social clubs you can join, too, but I imagine that would bore you to death. I belong to one, but it's too much drama and politics for me, and I could never stand that kind of thing. It's probably why I was a hair stylist for many years then opened the spa with my ex. I don't belong in corporate America, and neither does my big mouth."

Gage nods. "I hear ya. Me either. It's why I never went to college. I stayed on the ranch, learned to work the land and livestock as my father and granddaddy did before me. In my blood, I suppose."

"I think that's wonderful, Gage." I take a sip of my wine and hesitate with my next question. "Why did you leave it and come all the way across the country?"

He turns and grabs his beer, taking a long pull in one motion. He looks away into the darkening sky then back at me. His eyes seem far away as he takes a deep breath.

"I...uh...my wife died two years ago. Everything there is her. I hated coming home to nothing. I was getting drunk every night there for a while, just to get numb. And, you know, friends, relatives—they let you do your thing at first. They try to understand. Then the talks come into play. 'Time to pull it together, Gage,' they'd say, or 'You need to move on.' I'd known Jeanie since junior high. We got married right after high school."

He takes a few steps over to the grill and starts flipping the steaks and the random assortment of vegetables I'd found in my crisper. I don't know what to say. I feel so sad for him, but I have to know. He seems like such an open book and vulnerable right now, so I press gently with my next question.

"What did she die of, Gage?" I ask softly because I am afraid any loud noise might break him.

"Cancer. Breast." He spit the words out like poison. "Steaks are ready. Grab the plates."

I stand and take the plates over to him. He drops a steak on each plate and divides the peppers, mushrooms, and onions evenly between us. As we walk back over to the table and take our seats, I am choosing my next questions carefully, afraid he might get angry. I want to keep us talking. The conversation is real, just two friends shootin' the shit, both of us in comfortable clothes. Hell, I didn't even put makeup on. It's like one of the girls' nights, and it's great to talk to a man who isn't looking at you as a sex object.

"I'm so sorry that happened to you, Gage. Do you have children?"

He exhales loudly. "Nope. Jeanie wanted to wait and do a little community college first then work as a journalist at the local news office. By the time we tried, it wasn't happening, and then...cancer. She battled a good fight—four years—and then it just spread. I had to watch her get weaker and weaker. Felt so damned helpless."

"Gage, I'm truly sorry...and what about both your families?"

"Still there, her parents and mine. Like I said, it got to a point where no one could help, so I moved. I didn't start out with Florida in mind. I worked in just about every state from Montana to here. It's getting better, though. I like it here." He smiles

I smile back. "Good. I'm glad you do. I know life can be rough sometimes, but I'm certainly glad you came here. You definitely know what you're doing, and the horses have taken right to you."

He laughs a little soft laugh. "Well, I'm glad I could help. So, tell me where your lady friends are tonight."

I snort a laugh. "On dates."

"Why aren't you on a date?" He raises a questioning eyebrow.

"Oh, I date, I...just don't have one tonight is all."

"I see," he answers.

I roll my eyes. "Shut up and eat your steak."

"Oh, yes, ma'am."

* * *

Crystal.

This dude is a man-child...but legal. And I am having a wonderful evening despite the generational gap. We soon arrive at his swanky beachside apartment.

"Can I offer you a drink, Crystal? Wine? Champagne?"

"Geez, kid. Take it down a notch. Champagne? A bottle of water would be fine, thank you."

"Certainly. Would you mind if I have some wine?"

"Not at all," I assure him.

He puts on some music, slow rock from my era, and takes my hand to lead me to the sofa. He leans in for a kiss. *Oh, this poor kid. I'm going to break him.* He kisses me slowly, gently...which is just not gonna work. So I challenge him with my tongue and playfully bite his lip. Taking my hint, he gets more aggressive, and heavy breathing ensues. He pulls back for a moment and looks in my eyes.

"Bedroom?" he asks.

"Oh yes." I smile.

***

Renee.

I finally make it out of the house. While getting ready, I had to endure Maria's bossy demeanor and one of her lectures on how much my husband loves me. Jesus! No one is walking in my shoes. They all need to back off.

I spot the bar in the distance. As I drive closer, I see Steve wave from this big truck, and I pull into the spot next to it. He jumps out, and we stroll together into the place and get seated at a booth.

"Renee, you're looking sexy," he comments as he sits in the booth next to me, not across.

"Thanks." I stupidly giggle like a school girl.

"Do you mind if I sit next to you? It's so I can keep my hands on you," he whispers in my ear.

I look straight ahead as his hand covers my knee. I feel a little scared but somehow safe at the same time. "What movie did you have in mind tonight?" I ask, changing to a more normal conversation.

"I like all types of movies. Let's see what's playing after dinner and pick one then."

"Sounds good," I agree.

As we later drive to the theater, I think to myself that dinner went well. Feeling better about Steve after our conversation, I had decided to go in his truck with him. I enjoy listening to him talk about his work day and about his mother, who is widowed, and how he helps her from time to time. All normal life stuff. It relaxes me. I start to see there is a gentleman there, but he still plays the gigolo card.

Why? I wonder.

When the movie is over, he drives me back to my car. He holds the door for me as I step out of his truck, and then he's grabbing me, backing me up against the truck. Our mouths lock, and again his hands discover my body. He moves his tongue to my neck and up to my ear.

"Do you trust me?" he whispers.

"Yes..." I whisper back.

"Take me to your place."

I give him a serious look. I have two babies at home, sleeping. "What about your place?"

"No way. Not mine. I have a roommate you should not be subjected to."

I furrow my brows. "What?"

"Long story. Please—your place. I'll be quiet," he boyishly begs.

Every instinct in my body is warning me against it, but I give in. "Okay, Steve, but you'd better be a gentleman." I smile.

"Well, I should hope so. Look, I really like you; I'm not going to do anything you don't want."

CHAPTER 5

Dusty.

Today is going by fast, but not fast enough. I can't wait to get out of this grocery store and back home to wait for Crystal and Renee to come over. I want to know how their dates went. In the back of my head, I keep thinking about Gage. What a nice man. I feel sad about what he went through but glad he found me. He's just wonderful, and not bad to look at, but he works for me and he probably isn't interested in me, anyway.

I get home and put away groceries then chat with Gage again out by the paddocks. Suddenly, I realize the time has slipped away and the girls will be arriving soon.

Crystal and Renee show up at the same time, on time. "Come on in, girls!" I shout from the kitchen. "Red or white tonight?" I ask as they make their way in and plop down at my counter. "Wow, you both look exhausted! I hope that's a good sign," I say with a wink. I pour three glasses of a crisp chardonnay and hand one to each of my friends. "Well, I'm dying here, ladies. How did your dates go?"

"I'll go first," Rene offers, putting up her hand. "Let me see. Where do I start? Where I'm stupid...or a fool?"

We all quickly move to my living room and get comfortable, glasses in hand, as I ask anxiously, "What happened, Renee?"

Crystal squints at her. "What did you do?" she says with a smirk.

"Okay, don't judge. We took it back to my house last night."

"Renee!" I yell. "That was against the rules. No men back to our houses!"

"I know, I know, but Steve's all right. He's not really disrespectful, and I am an adult. He spent the night, BUT we didn't sleep together...Well, we didn't have intercourse, anyway."

"Details, girlfriend," Crystal says calmly.

"So, we go to dinner and a movie. I gotta say, the whole time he's with me he is always touching me, but not in a bad way. You know...holding hands, sitting next to me in a booth. At the movies, he picked up my legs and threw them over his and he just caressed them. It was sweet."

"That's called buttering you up," I say sarcastically.

"Yes, I suppose it is, but I liked the attention."

"Go ahead," Crystal prods. "What happened? How'd you end up at your place?"

"When I asked him about his place, he said he has a roommate I should not be subjected to. My first thought is he's married."

We look at Renee with eyes as wide as golf balls.

"He said he's not, but I don't know if I believe him. Anyway, then we made out on the couch like teenagers. That was fun, but things got intense, so we went off to the guest room. I kept him downstairs to not disturb the girls. Didn't want to wake them or Maria. He then tells me he wants to go slow, wants to make me feel good, so he slips off my pants but leaves his on. And proceeds to go down on me. Girls, oh...my...God. I have no clue who taught this man the things he did with his tongue, but he made me orgasm two friggin' times! Even thinking about it now is gonna set me off."

We stare at Renee as we each take a big gulp of our wine and are noticeably breathing heavily along with her.

"I did reciprocate, of course."

We lean in, eyes wide.

"He dropped his pants and the woody that sprang forward...well, I don't think I ever saw one that big."

"So you blew him?" Crystal asks in an excited tone.

"Yes, and he barely fit in my mouth. Then we just talked all night. He left at about four a.m. That's why I look tired. And I'm not sure how I feel about all this."

I lean my head to the side and give Renee an understanding look. "Okay, as I see it, you are separated. Did you have fun, and did it feel good?"

"Oh yeah."

"Then just let it be. I guess it's good he didn't leave right after."

"I agree with Dusty, Renee. But I'm still wondering, if he's married and cheating, why wouldn't he want to fuck your brains out?"

"I know, and he could have taken advantage of the situation. He is stronger and bigger. But he was actually gentle, and if I told him to slow down, he did. I haven't heard from him at all today, though. So typical."

"It's okay, Renee. Don't get attached. He's what they call a *fuck boy*," I say, gazing next at Crystal, who is sitting a little too quietly. "So...your turn, now. How did the date with college boy go?"

Crystal picks up her wine glass, takes a big mouthful of the chardonnay, and swallows hard. "All right, this might bring down our high from Renee's story. The date went off perfectly. For a young guy, he has his shit together. He's your typical rich kid, had it easier because of his parents, but I don't have a problem with that. I had the same advantages. He's successful in his own right. Works hard and runs a business, from the sounds of it. So, we went back to his place, and the sex was great. I mean it's awesome being with a younger man, because he kept up with me better. He had me going in so many directions. Flipped me all over the bed. I felt like I was in the Kama Sutra. I think we could have done it twice, but after he came the first time, I wasn't sticking around for another show."

Renee looks up from her glass. "What? Why?"

"Girls, I have never seen what I'm about to tell you. He wore a condom, but right before he was going to come, he pulled out, pulled off the condom, and ejaculated all over my breasts."

Renee and I wrinkle our eyebrows together. "Yeah...so?" we say in unison.

Crystal sits up straight, "Then he licked it off."

I put my hand over my nose and mouth so I won't vomit. I toss Renee a glance and see her face is contorted as if she smells or tastes something bad. "Wait a minute," I chime in. "He licked his own jizz?"

Crystal nods once. "Oh yeah. And he was into it."

Renee starts to laugh. "Holy shit. What did you do?"

"I let him finish his snack and I got up, got dressed, thanked him for a great evening, and dashed out the door."

I made a vomit sound as we all kind of laughed. "Well, that's...uh...interesting."

"Damn. I don't think I would have been as calm as you, Crystal. I think I would have just shouted, 'What the fuck?'"

I agree and take another big gulp of wine as silence hangs in our atmosphere while we try to absorb the situation poor Crystal had to endure.

To change our thoughts, I pick up the bowl of chips and ask, "Does anyone want some dip?"

Not a good idea just yet.

* * *

Crystal.

Sunday passes as I watch one movie after another. Jason, a.k.a. Jizz Licker, texts me a few times, but I can't bring myself to reply. I just can't.

On a good note, my mother calls.

"Hi, Mom."

"Bonjour, mon coeur."

I smile in delight that she is this happy all the time. "Mom, please just speak in English."

"Ahhh...*oui*. I met a wonderfully handsome gentleman yesterday. He is single, he is sophisticated, he is your age. An American. His name is Henry Malbeck, sort of like the wine. His work is in the States and here. He's a big attorney of some sort. Has a little condo here on the Riviera and a home in Lake Tahoe, California. He loves to ski. I showed him your picture, and he said how gorgeous you are and asked if he could meet you."

"MOM!" I squealed. "I don't know if I'm flattered or pissed."

"What, *mon ange*? I am trying to help you. You must trust me."

"I do trust you, Mom, but seriously, I have a life here in Florida. How do you suppose this is going to work?"

"Ahh, details. Nothing for young people like you and him with money."

"Do you have a picture of him?" I interrogate.

"Mmm...but of course. I'll send it when I get off the phone."

Suddenly, I'm thankful I taught Mom how to use her iPhone. "Great. Send it, and I'll let you know what I think."

"*Oui*. You will call him or text him. I know what you like. Trust me, Henry is a man's man. He looks like a movie star."

"Bye, Mom. Send the picture and let me be the judge."

"*Au revoir, mon ange*. Talk to you during the week."

I wasn't off the phone a minute when the photo came in. "Holy hotness!" Chiseled chin; dark, wavy hair; dark-blue eyes. Just a dream. Then the next text from Mom comes in with a phone number and:

Make the call, he said, only if you're interested.

I know you are. Love, Mom.

***

Dusty.

"Could you show me again how you did that with Ariel?" I ask Gage. He is teaching the horses to ground tie and, when they are being mounted, to stand still until the rider gives the cue to move forward. He is wonderful with my animals, giving them the consistent discipline they need while still being light-handed and calm with them. I can tell they have a certain respect for him because of this, too.

Gage works with me and Ariel for a while, showing me how to give her firm but quiet voice commands and to make sure her attention is on me and not everything else around us. When he is satisfied we have done enough with that, he gets on Jeremial and we take the two horses out for a ride across the fields.

When we return, we groom and exercise Miguel and Chamuel, as well. As Gage is finishing the barn chores, I invite him up to the house to watch a football game. His eyes go wide. "You like football?" he asks in disbelief.

"Of course. I could not grow up in a house with my dad and brothers and not like football."

"Well, Miss Dusty, I'm going to have to say yes to that. Thank you very much."

"Great! Game starts at four. Just come on in through the kitchen door, grab a beer, and get your game face on."

Gage tips his hat. "See ya at four."

***

Renee.

While the girls spend the day with Frank, I pour a cup of coffee and surf the Blind Date site. I see Steve is online. This makes me hurt a little inside. I know I should not get too attached to him; he's probably making other dates. But I send him a text in his message box anyway.

Hey—what ya doing?

Immediately he's off the grid and my cell phone dings with him texting me.

Nothing. What are you doing?

I shake my head.

Clearing losers' messages out of my box. Men are pigs sometimes.

No, they want to have fun. You need to get a thicker skin if you're gonna be on here.

There must be good men on here. I really don't need to see dick pictures along with porn talk when I don't even know them.

It's a game, sweetie. You should know how to play it.

I guess I don't know how. Besides, I'm a mother of two girls, and a lot of these men are so disrespectful. I won't put up with it.

You let me have fun.

I almost choke on my coffee as tears well up in my eyes.

I suppose I guessed wrong about you then. Have fun finding a whore to play with.

What? Hey, I'm sorry. I was joking with you. I do respect you. You are a bit of a princess, though, and you do have to be careful. No worries with me. Did you feel I used you?

Not sure now.

Maybe you used me. It's okay—we're adults. Consenting adults. I would never push you to do anything. Sorry if you feel otherwise.

I leave that final text alone and don't reply. I let some tears fall, but really, I shouldn't be hurt. I knew what I was walking into, going on a date with Steve. He is nice and treated me very well, but he must do that with two or three girls a week.

Hey, can I see you this weekend?

I stare at his next text in disbelief. I can tell this is an "Uh oh, I might have blown it!" text.

Maybe. Let me see how my week goes, I respond.

You let me know, princess. Just call me.

*****

Dusty.

Just before four, I click on the T.V. The game should start after the news. I hear the back-door opening followed by a slight whistle.

"Miss Dusty?" Gage yells.

"Yep, come on in. Grab a beer out of the refrigerator and come inside." I hear him go through the motions, and finally he's walking into my living room.

He raises his beer and opens another as he hands it to me. "Here ya go."

"Thanks, Gage." We clink them together and collapse onto the sofa. "The game is on right after the news."

Gage points with his bottle of beer at the screen. "Did they catch this creep yet?"

Confused, I look back at the screen. Seems the sledgehammer rapist is at it again. "Oh no! He killed another woman?"

"Yeah," Gage says, "right over in Poinciana Park."

"Wow, he's getting closer. He's hit Knoll Ridge, the Landings, and now Poinciana. I hope they catch him soon."

Gage gives me a long look like he's wanting to ask me something, so I take the pressure off him. "What?" I say simply.

"Do you have a gun?"

"Yes, but it's a shotgun for here at the farm."

"That's the only one you have?"

"Yes. Why?"

"With this creep going around, you might want to get one you can carry."

I eye him thoughtfully. "I have thought about it. My girlfriend Crystal has one in her purse. I never really thought I needed to until now."

"You might want to check about carrying one, at least until this piece of shit is caught."

"I think I might," I answer.

The game starts, and after a few moments, I glance in Gage's direction. "How do you feel about pizza?"

"It's one of my favorite food groups."

I laugh. "And how do you feel about meat on it? Bacon? Pepperoni? Sausage? Meatballs?"

He smiles wide. "All of it."

I nod affirmatively, pick up my cell, and order for delivery.

CHAPTER 6

Crystal.

I hesitate about calling Henry, but then I give myself the pep talk: "I am a strong, independent woman who can call a guy if I want." After all, he said to call him if I am interested. I suppose that could be considered the first move, but nice way to put the ball in my court. *Shit!*

I tap the numbers. He answers on the first ring.

"Hello."

"Hi, is this Henry?"

"Yes, it is. Is this Crystal?"

"Yes, but how did you know it was me?"

"Your mother is a fascinating woman. She told me you would call, and I had no choice but to believe her. I must say I am glad you did."

I feel my face get hot at the sound of his strong, smooth voice.

I smile. "Yes, my mother can be a little bit pushy. Sorry about that."

"I'm not," he says, and I can tell he is smiling, too. "Tell me, Crystal, where in Florida are you?"

"Fort Lauderdale. I've been here for almost twelve years."

We continue to talk for over an hour about everything—likes, dislikes, our careers, family, and lifestyle—and discover we have much in common.

Before we hang up, he informs me, "I truly enjoyed talking with you. You sound like a fascinating woman! And I look forward to our next chat. May I call you in a day or two?"

"Of course. That would be very nice."

As I climb into bed that night with my laptop, I check the *Blind Date* site. One after another, I see messages from these fucking idiot men with their nasty sexual behaviors. I thought I could really have some fun, and I know I could if I wanted to play it their way, but some of these guys are just plain nasty. *Especially this one that constantly leaves messages to suck his balls. He must be a real charmer.* I shut it down with a laugh then realize what a great conversation I had with Henry. How normal it was and easy, like I'd known him for years.

                            ***

Renee.

My cell chimes at six a.m. It's Steve,
telling me he is on the road and working
already. I ignore the message and get up to
take care of my girls and get one off to
preschool. It's a rainy, damp Monday. I send
a two-way text to Crystal and Dusty, asking
them if they could do lunch because I just
feel like I need to be around friends today.
Thankfully, they agree.

It's about noon when the girls stroll in to
the little beachside café. This place is small
and quiet and only open till two p.m., just a
breakfast/lunch kind of place. The beach is
empty, and the silvery sky cracks with
lightning and a low groan of thunder. The
server steps over to us and asks, "The usual,
girls?" We nod. She knows us and soon brings
us iced tea and the salads we always order.

"So, what's up, Renee? Feeling like the
weather?" Dusty asks.

"I suppose," I answer with a sigh. "It's this
Steve guy. I could really be into him, but
there is something there I'm not sure of."

"He's a player," Crystal snaps. "Just don't let him in. Let me guess—you caught him in a lie or something and he tried to make it better...where before you didn't hear from him, and then he's calling you or texting you every day."

I roll my eyes and exhale loudly out of my nose like a dragon. "Holy shit. Yes! I didn't hear from him after we did our little oral sexcapades, then I saw him online, trolling the dating site. We texted back and forth, not so pleasantly, and now he texted me this morning, telling me he's at work, et cetera, like we are in a good relationship or something. I can't read him at all."

"Yep. Fuck boy. Crystal's right; play back and just have fun with it. Stop yourself from getting attached. It's been a long time for you. I had a feeling you might have gotten hooked on the first guy that gave you some attention."

I nod at Dusty. She's right. "Why can't I just play the game? You know, that's what he said, too—it's a game. Well, I don't get this game."

Crystal holds up a bread stick and points it at me. "You don't understand it because you're not the type. I was, but I'm tired." She bites the stick in half. "Have you all seen the messages in our *Blind Date* in-box? Holy crap, it's like a porno. I mean, I get the sex part of this, but right out of the gate, these guys start with 'suck my balls' and 'I'll lick you till you pass out.' At least let's meet first. Geez."

Dusty looks up from her chicken Caesar. "Yes, I've been reading those, too. Have guys changed that much? I thought this would be fun, but the messages are mostly gross. There are only a few nice ones. Meanwhile, I gotta tell ya: someone going down on me till I pass out sounds good, but yes, I would like dinner first."

Our laughter is so loud the waitress wants to know what was so funny. Which makes us laugh even more. She walks away, chuckling at us and shaking her head.

"So, my mother kind of set me up with this really nice guy. I have to show you his picture." Crystal starts swiping her phone and then shows us this hunk of a man.

Dusty and I gawk over the photo. "Have you talked with him already?" I ask.

"Yes. He's very sweet, and our conversation was actually stimulating. It's nice to have a normal talk—you know, not perverted or trying to put the moves on you, asking what color your underwear is or how much cock you can fit in your mouth. Just normal. He wanted to know about me, to get to know me to see if we would be compatible, and so far, it seems like we might very well be a good fit."

I smile at Crystal. She looks happy, almost giddy. "That's wonderful."

"When are you going to meet him?" Dusty asks.

"Not sure, yet. He said he'd call me in a day or so. Since we live across the country from one another, I guess it will take some figuring out. We'll just have to wait and see." She shrugs.

"Speaking of hunks, how's that sexy ranch hand working out, Dusty?" Crystal adds.

Dusty's laugh is throaty and low. "He's a nice guy. Might have some past baggage. And, like your Henry, we have had decent conversations. Nothing flirty—he does work for me—but a gentleman; I will say that."

I tilt my head. "What kind of baggage? We all have baggage."

Dusty's face winces a bit. "The kind that comes with a dead wife. And a family that can't help his pain. So he's been on the move from Montana for a year or so, working where he can. That kind of baggage."

"Christ," I say softly. "That's sad baggage."

"Yeah, tell me about it, but you should see him with my horses. The man is like the horse whisperer, and...it's hot."

"Did you make a date with Carlos yet?"

"Yep, chatted with him earlier. We are on for this Friday night," Dusty says.

We finish our meals, pay the check, then dash to our cars because it is now pouring again. I shout as we sprint through the parking lot, "Saturday night? My house?"

My friends give me their thumbs up, and off we go, back to jobs, homes, and kids.

***

Dusty.

As I pull up my long driveway, I wonder what Gage is up to on this stormy day. I park and head quickly to the house. I don't see him out back, so I grab an umbrella before stomping across the yard to the stable. And there he is, brushing Ariel. I just watch for a minute, getting lost in my thoughts. The other horses have their sheets over them. It's calm, cozy, and warm in the barn, and this guy is amazing. For a second, I'm almost dizzy. I feel the ground move a little and vibrate my feet in a good way. Gage calls my name and it zaps me back.

"Hey, Dusty. Home already?"

I blink, smile, and focus. His voice pulls me further back out of my mind. "Yes, it was only lunch. How's the troops?"

"The horses, if that's what you mean, are just fine." He bunches his eyebrows and lifts his chin. "You all right? You look a little off."

"Oh. Uh...yeah. I'm good. I think I'm a little under the weather is all."

I follow my words with a smile, trying to hide my awkwardness. I think I'm having feelings for him. But I'm afraid of it. Who is he, really? And with the past he's running from, I'm sure he does not want to get involved at all. If I make the first move, he might quit. And I can't risk that. My horses have never been so cared for. He literally talks to them.

"I'm going to go inside for a while. Let me know if you need me."

Gage nods and waves the brush. I walk back to the house, feeling empty inside. I decide to take a hot shower and check the *Blind Date* site for a chuckle.

But what I find is not what I call humorous. What a horror show of men. Some even start out very nice then after a few minutes of talking to them, they want to know your sexual fantasies or how you like to take it. I thought this would be fun, but it's so obvious times have changed. *Where are the gentlemen?*

I get a message again from Carlos, asking if we are still on for our date. I confirm that we are and tell him where I'll meet him. The good news so far with this guy is he has never been inappropriate. Needy, maybe, but not perverted.

* * *

Crystal.

Arriving back at my office, I see my secretary, Meredith, has a sneaky smile on her face as I walk past her desk. I glance back at her then stop and turn on my heel.

"What's with the look? What are you up to?"

She stands, her smile smug as she steps over to my door and opens it. "Maybe I should be asking you what you've been up to."

I look at her curiously and then catch sight of what is perched on my desk: a dozen white and yellow roses in a clear vase with a white bow. "Are those for me?" I ask.

"Yes, and I'm dying. Who are they from?"

I step up to my desk. "I have no idea."

Meredith moves next to me, spewing enthusiasm. "Read the card!"

I take the little envelope and pull out the message to read it aloud. "Thank you for a delightful conversation last night. Thought about you all night long. I'll call you later. Henry."

I am stunned, frozen in place. I can't remember a time any man was this thoughtful.

"So, who the hell is Henry?" Meredith blurts.

I look at her, bewildered.

"Whoa, look at your face. Crystal, who's Henry!"

I walk around the desk to sit down. Meredith takes the seat across from me. "I had a two-, maybe three-hour conversation with him last night on the phone. He's a man my mother met and thought I would like. He lives in Lake Tahoe, California, and flies back and forth to France for work."

"Was last night the first time you guys spoke?" she questions.

I nod my head, my eyes wide in disbelief.

"Really. Hey, can your mom set me up with someone like him, too?"

I burst into laughter. "She probably can!"

***

Renee.

My day is moving along. I haven't heard from Steve since early yesterday morning. The smart part of my brain says, "Shut off the phone and don't touch it." The idiot part says, "Oh, just send him a text. See what he's up to." Ignoring the better advice, the idiot part wins the battle.

Hey. How's your day going?

He doesn't answer right away. In fact, he doesn't answer till five in the afternoon. And all it says is:

Busy day.

"REALLY?" I shout at my phone. My kids turn around from watching cartoons and eye me for second. The older one shrugs at the baby, and they go back to watching their annoying show.

I feel my stomach turn. My eyes start to well up while I try to talk myself off the ledge. In my head, I repeat, *You're a grown-ass woman. What are crying about? You're separated, you have kids, you had a nice fling with a hot guy. Now move it on.*

The tears come down anyway. I stomp up the stairs to my bedroom, where I can let it out and not worry the girls. I need to be held. Oddly, I almost feel as though I should call Frank. But tell him what? That I'm dating this hot guy and he's playing head games with me? Part of me tells myself, *If Steve really wanted me, he would be here, or at least I wouldn't be so confused.*

My phone vibrates. It's Dusty. I hesitate but decide to answer. My voice cracks as I say hello.

"Renee? Oh, honey, are you crying?"

I stay silent as more tears flush from my eyes.

"Renee!" Dusty speaks more firmly. "Are you okay? Are the kids okay?"

"Yes...yes, I'm fine. Just a bad day is all."

"You're not fine. What's wrong, sweetie? What happened?"

I sniff. "I don't know, Dusty. Maybe I'm not supposed to do this. I can't date. I really like Steve, but I can't make him want me the same way, and now I feel foolish for being intimate with him. And what's worse, for some strange reason I feel like I need Frank to hold me."

"Shhh...okay, Renee. Just breathe. First things first. Bottom line, Steve is for fun, he plays the field, and you're not going to change him. Agree?"

"Yes."

"There you go. Just think of him as a check mark on your list. Fooled around with hot stud...check! Now put it aside and go on another date. There are plenty of fish to hook. Try another. Maybe talk to one for a while before you meet him, get to know him a little better. Try feeling him out. As for needing a hug from Frank, I get it. You've been married to him for years; he was always there to kiss your proverbial boo-boos; he's the father of your children. And as one of your best friends, I say you shouldn't push him aside. Get over whatever it is you're going through. I'm telling you, it's depression. You don't see it, but we do, and trust me, we are keeping a watch on you. Just live your life; stop worrying about men. Time and a place for everything, right? Things will happen when they are supposed to."

I remain quiet. She's right. But I don't like it, and I am so confused. But, God dammit, she's right. Am I depressed? Are my hormones making me crazy? I don't feel crazy, but here I am, crying on the phone over a man I hardly know.

"Feel better, sweetie?"

"A little. Thank you. You're right. I'm just gonna back off and breathe. Take this time to sort stuff out."

"There you go, and don't overthink this dating thing. If you can't do it, don't. But if you do, remember: it's for fun, just like the guys do it. Honestly, you think Steve is sitting around wondering what you're doing? No, and some other woman probably has her legs wrapped around his neck tonight."

I laugh. "Oh God, that makes me sick." But I keep laughing at Dusty's blunt description, and her deep laugh mixes with my giggles.

"I'm glad I could help. Have a nice night with your babes. Then go play online and move that fabulous ass around."

I'm still in giggles as I get off the cell. It's so stupid. Really, I'm acting ridiculous. But if Steve would call me right now, I know I'd drop and run. How sad is that?

The rest of the night, I have fun making mac n' cheese and watching *The Secret Life of Pets* with my girls. All too soon it's time for bed. After a while, they finally settled and drifted off to sleep. By this time, it's ten p.m. I too should go to bed, but I pour myself a steep glass of wine, sit at my computer, and hunt around the *Blind Date* site. Dusty was right—we have a lot of hits on here. I log into the messages and start to read them one at a time.

I must admit, I am happy that Steve is not online, but it does not mean he's sucking face or whatever with someone else. Again, that thought makes me sad. I shake my head. *Stop it!*

I click the message button. Quite a few prospects, I see. I check the first one.

Hey, baby! Here's my digits. Let's chat.

"Okay, that would be a no. Next."

Hello, Anna. I've got a big cock. Want to take bets it doesn't fit anywhere? Lol!!

A big giggle-snort comes out of me as I shake my head. I truly don't understand what these guys are thinking. So many have the same lines. Must be a male thing, or an asshole-male thing. My husband would never talk like that. Or I should hope he wouldn't.

I sip at my chardonnay and keep scanning and deleting, weeding out what seems to be one dirt bag after the other. Then, finally I stumble on a message that seems almost timid and endearing.

Hello, Anna. I don't know if I'm doing this right. Forgive me if I sound like a complete idiot. This is all new to me. I read your profile. You sound normal. Can we meet? G.W.

"How sweet." *At last*, I thought. *A decent man.* I quickly respond:

Hi, G.W. Nice to hear from you. How do you feel about having a few chats on the phone to get to know one another before we have a date?

Within about three minutes, I have an answer.

Sounds good to me. Here's my number.

I answer him with a *Thank You* and ask if it's too late to call right now. He says,

Fine—go ahead and give me a jingle.

How cute, I think. *Who says 'jingle'?*

Maybe a little too excitedly, I dial.

"Hello, is this Anna?"

"Yes, it is. Hello, G.W."

"Hi there. You may call me G."

"Hi, G. Thanks for letting me call. I'm not doing very well on this dating site. There are a lot of men that are just pigs and say disgusting things."

"Yep, you gotta be careful. I don't blame ya one bit, there."

We talk for about a half hour. His voice is a little raspy with a Southern twang. He is from the area and works in construction. I tell him I have two small girls but neither of us give each other too much personal info. He is very laid back, easygoing. Never once does he say anything inappropriate or even use any foul language, for that matter. I can tell he is trying to be a real gentleman. His laugh is kind and sort of contagious. He also seems to have a good sense of humor.

Before we hang up, he confirms this is my cell number and tells me he'll call me tomorrow or the day after so we can continue to chat until I feel comfortable enough to meet him.

After I get off the phone with him, I go right to bed. I let his words wash over me, roll around. I go over the conversation in my mind. I know I'm over-analyzing; I don't know why I am. As drowsiness starts to relax me, I think, *Thank God I finally got a nice one.*

Suddenly, I'm startled by the chime, a text notification. I roll over and check it. Steve wrote:

Good night. Sweet dreams.

"HA! Are you kidding me?" I say aloud at my phone. *What is it with this guy? I haven't heard a peep from him and now an unexpected 'good night'?* I throw my phone down and don't respond. *Unbelievable. I'm so done.*

CHAPTER 7

Dusty.

All night long, Renee is on my mind. I am a little worried about her emotional state. I don't think I have ever heard her cry so much or be so confused.

In the morning, I grab a mug and pour myself some coffee, sipping it as I walk outside to the back patio. Thoughts of Gage getting up super early, letting himself in, and starting the coffee make me smile.

I get comfortable in my outdoor rocking chair in time to see Gage. I hold up my mug as a good-morning-thanks-for-the-brew gesture. He gives his cowboy hat a slight tip.

He's so sweet.

I then make a call to Crystal.

"What's up, Dusty? You only call this early when you're worried about something. Wait—let me get some coffee in me."

I hear her gulp a few times. "Okay, lay it on me."

"Well, it's Renee," I say flatly

"I think I already know, but go ahead," she urges.

"She's very emotional. Last night, we were on the phone and she was crying over Steve but wanting to call Frank and cry to him and have him hold her. She didn't just cry, either—she ugly cried. I'm concerned. Maybe she shouldn't do this dating thing. Maybe we should encourage her to get some counseling."

"I know." Crystal sighs heavily. "She isn't going to listen to us, though. The only thing I can think of is to watch her closely, maybe find out when she's on a date. Then we can either happen to be there or at least not be far."

"Well, there is Frank," I say matter-of-factly.

"Yeah, what about him?"

"We all know he is not going away. He is gonna stay and fight for her, so maybe we should tell him how unstable she is and that we are worried about her."

"Dusty, I think he already knows; he's not stupid. Renee has a good man there. She just has to get through whatever her hormones are doing. But if you feel in your heart you need to talk to Frank, then call him."

"I just might. See what he has to say about it."

"Let me know what you decide. I've got to jump in the shower, shave, shampoo. Not necessarily in that order, but I have work to do and I'll be in court this week. People are paying me a lot of money to get their divorces through."

I laugh. "Thanks for the heads up! Go on— have a good day with your fabulous ass. Chat later."

I end the call with Crystal, and Gage steps from out of nowhere and startles me. "Gage! I didn't see you."

"Oh, sorry about that. I heard you on the phone, not really eavesdropping, but I didn't want to interrupt. I just wanted to know if you would like to take a ride up to the feed and tack store. The feed I ordered is in. Also, there's some saddles I want you to look at."

"Okay, sure. I'll have to go shower and make myself presentable, but first I want to finish this wonderful coffee."

"You look all right to me. Just throw on some jeans and a T-shirt and let's go. I'll take ya for breakfast. My treat."

"I look all right? Have you been in the sun too much? I at least must do something with my hair, wash my face, put on mascara and lipstick. If not, people will talk, thinking I've gone crazy!" I laugh and shake my head.

"See, here's where you women get it all wrong. You don't have any idea how adorable you look when you get up in the morning. Face all tired like a cute little child, hair all messy, face not made up with all that paint like a mannequin. It's just not normal. Y'all are pretty without the fuss."

I stare at him for a moment. He's all smiles and bright eyes, but I can only smirk and scoff at him. "I have to stop by the spa first."

"Come on then, lady. Drink up. We're burnin' daylight."

***

Crystal.

The law firm is all kinds of fucked up this morning. Mid-week, and shit's hitting the fan. Meredith scheduled four different clients today, and I have got to get ready for court tomorrow, though she says she has me covered. Other partners in the firm keep coming and going in and out of my office like I'm the fucking genie with all the answers.

It's noon on the dot, and I'm pleasantly surprised to see Henry is calling.

"Hello! What makes me so lucky?" I answer my cell with laughter.

"Hey, how's your day going?"

I sigh.

"Ouch! That bad?"

His voice is soothing, like cold water going down a burning, parched throat. Henry, being a fellow attorney, understands the nightmare I'm going through today with work.

"Just breathe. Nothing can get done unless you focus. When I see you, we'll talk about how to invent a less hectic environment for work, though you do work in a firm that deals with many factors. Tell me, did you ever consider branching out on your own, taking a few clients for higher fees so you can focus on just the ones you want rather than ones thrown at you and spread around?"

"Well, of course, yes, but it took me a long time to get here. I don't really want to start over. My fiftieth birthday is looming, so I don't take too many chances with my career right now."

"I understand. When I see you, we'll talk. That's part of the reason for this phone call, by the way. I can fly you out here, or I can come to Florida week after next. I was thinking a long weekend, maybe. What are your thoughts? I don't want to impose."

I quickly look at my schedule and see a few appointments that I'll have Meredith move up. In my head, I roughly go over things, *I'll work through next weekend, move Thursday to Wednesday, and make it work.*

"Yes, I can move my appointments around. So we're talking Thursday, the eighteenth?"

"Yes. Would you like for me to come to you?"

"That would be great, Henry. I'm looking forward to meeting you."

"And I am looking forward to meeting you as well, Crystal. Have a good lunch, breathe deep, and don't work too hard. I'll call you in a day or two. But hey, if you need to talk and de-stress in the meantime, I'd love to help."

"Thank you. It certainly beats screaming my head off. I scare the help when I do that."

His laugh is hearty as he says goodbye. I just sit there in a harmonious glow. The effect he has on me is calming. I just want more. I grab my little half of a turkey sandwich and pour a small glass of pinot grigio. I ease back in my desk chair and swivel around till I'm looking out my floor-to-ceiling windows in my beautiful office, the one I fought for that was so hard to get. I take the deep breath Henry prescribed and stare out over the Atlantic Ocean. I see sunbathers, people sailing, and swimmers. I think of my boat and daydream about taking Henry out for a cruise on it.

My beautiful reverie is soon violated by a knock at my door and Meredith's voice asking me yet another question. I don't turn, and I don't respond.

"Crystal, do you hear me? Harrison and Ward. Line two."

Still facing the ocean, I hold my glass above my head. It's all she can see. Firmly but pleasantly I reply, "Do you see this?"

"Yesss…"

"It's fucking lunch time. I'm on fucking lunch. I'll call them back in forty-five fucking minutes."

"Okay—got it. And are you okay?"

"I will be as soon as I can have some peace and quiet, some lunch, and some fucking air."

"Got it. Is this a new thing? Because it's about fucking time."

"Yes, for the love of God and my sanity, we will now have an hour lunch and quite possibly a three-p.m. glass of wine. And I'll be off on a long weekend Thursday the eighteenth. I'll work through next weekend, so make that happen. Move stuff; get rid of shit; I don't care. But I need that weekend badly.

"Hmmm...would this have anything to do with a particular man named Henry?"

"Yes. It. Does."

"Good. You deserve it. I'll wake you up from this bliss at one o'clock."

"Meredith?"

"Yeah?"

"Make it one-fifteen."

"No problem."

***

Renee.

It's one of those mornings—or should I say afternoons, now? I got up, got the little ones ready with the help of my nanny, and then climbed back into bed. I feel so blue. I'm crying for no reason...or many. I sit up in my bed and grab the laptop to search for G.W.

95

Hey, are you there?

It takes about five minutes for him to answer.

I'm here. What's up? You doing okay?

I'm okay, I guess. Just a little down.

Oh, I'm sorry. How can I help cheer you up, Anna?

I smile.

I believe you already are. You at least brought a smile to my face by asking.

Oh good. That wasn't too hard. Maybe you just need a friend to talk to. Do you have girlfriends?

Yes, but they are busy.

Well, I hope we are becoming friends. You can talk to me. I'll listen.

It's funny, but for some reason that's all I needed. Someone to talk to who really didn't know me that well. Funny how it's easier sometimes to talk to almost complete strangers and feel better, maybe because they judge less? Or don't really care as much? Whatever it is, G.W. is fulfilling that need, and after texting for an hour he gives in and calls me.

Our conversation lasts for hours more, during which he makes me laugh several times. He's very down to earth, and his raspy voice is becoming endearing. I tell him just enough as not to get in too deep with him, yet. He also tells me of past relationships and a marriage that went bad. He even mentions his mom and how he helps her every now and again because his dad passed on.

By the time we say goodbye, he asks me if I am feeling better. Truth be told, I am.

"See now?" he says. "You just needed a little chat with a friend. Glad I could help you out. Oh, and Anna, no rush. I don't want you to feel any pressure about it, but when you are more comfortable, you let me know when you'd like to go on a date."

I told him I'd let him know. So thoughtful. I like that he is taking his time with me.

The rest of the day, I feel much better and take a book outside to the pool, figuring some sun will do me good.

* * *

Dusty.

After my talk with Crystal, I get myself together and follow Gage to the feed store, then I go to spend the rest of the morning at my spa. My manager, Robin, has the place open and everything in order. We go over supplies and payroll then set up meetings and appointments. I tell her I am taking the afternoon off for an early date with someone I've met online.

"Have fun, but please be careful. I did that online dating shit, too. I don't doubt there are probably some decent guys on there, but the majority are pervs. Have you gotten dick pictures yet?" She rolls her eyes in disgust.

I glare back at her with the same eyes. "YES!" I squeal. "Please tell me what on earth they are thinking. I don't even know these men, and they send pictures of their junk and want you to do the same? Like that's going to make me say, 'Oh hey, baby, I want to meet you!'"

Robin laughs in agreement. "Unfortunately, I think there are women out there who are that desperate. One time, I was interested enough just to see what kind of asshole this one guy was and how far I could push him, so I played with his mind a little and agreed to talk with him on the phone. After a few times, he seemed normal, but then every so many days—BOOM! He would send me a dick pic and say, 'Are you ready for Mr. Happy?'" She makes a gagging sound. "So, when I finally said okay to a date, he said, 'Never mind. We are not a good match.' That was his answer because he knew I was not going to fuck him on a first date. Just be careful. I know you're no dummy."

I listen to her story and just shake my head. "Jesus, what the hell is wrong with these idiots? I swear, are there any real gentlemen out there?"

"Yeah, they are there," she assures. "Sometimes right under our noses."

I get up from my desk, purse and keys in hand. "Thanks, Robin. I'll let you know how it goes."

"Like I said, be careful. Tell friends where you are so they can be around in case of trouble. Hell, you can call me, too. It's scary out there, and they still haven't caught that crazy sledgehammer rapist."

I turn back to face her in the doorway. "He's still out there? I haven't been paying attention to the news. They haven't caught him yet?"

She shrugs. "Nope."

"I do carry mace; all my friends do. I'll make sure I always have it with me."

When I arrive home, all my horses are out in the field. What a beautiful afternoon for a ride. *I'll go in, change my clothes, and saddle up one of my babies,* I tell myself.

Out at the stable, Gage is there working his ass off. I swear I've never had someone this capable, and it makes me feel even more reassured.

"Hey, Gage, I thought I'd take a ride."

He nods at Chamuel. "She could use some exercise along with Miguel. I'll go with you unless you want to be alone."

"No...uh, that's fine. We can do the trails over by the park."

"Great. I'll help ya with the new saddle."

I watch Gage take his time and tack the horses up with such care. He calmly and quietly talks to them as his hands move with a steady confidence. With each horse, he makes sure all parts of the saddle and bridle are fitting properly and not pinching or rubbing the horse's body. I am impressed by how the horses stand patiently while he works with them.

"You're so good with them, Gage. They were never this well behaved for anyone, including me."

"It's all in the attitude. They are stronger and bigger, and they know it. But they know we might be a little smarter. So, you've gotta let them know you're like the alpha mare or stallion of the herd. They start to trust you as a leader. And your confidence gives them confidence, especially when trying new things."

"How did you get so smart at this?" I ask.

"Smart?" he quips. "Nope, you just have to observe them, almost listen to them, in a way, like we were talking about before. It's not that hard, but it does take a long time and a lot of practice. Fortunately, I grew up with it and learned from some of the best horsemen around—my daddy and granddaddy."

I climb on to Chamuel as Gage mounts Miguel. Off we ride onto the trail. We are quiet for most of the journey, just taking in the beautiful day. The sun peeks in and out from behind white clouds as the cool breeze makes for low humidity. The horses even seem to be more alert on this clear day. Finally, through the woods of the trail, we can smell the salt air of the coast in the distance.

"Have you ever taken the horses over to the beach to ride?" Gage asks, breaking one of our silent stretches.

"A couple of times. They love the water, but the town isn't pleased with bringing big animals onto their pristine beaches."

He gives me a devilish look. "Well, what do you say? I'm game if you are."

"I like the way you think, Gage."

We urge Miguel and Chamuel toward the road. They are somewhat accustomed to traffic, but we are still cautious with them and need to calm them a bit. Finally, some cars stop to let us cross to the small wooden bridge leading to the beach path. The horses pick their way carefully across the planks, but after they've stepped onto the sandy pathway, we cue them into a trot and head straight for the surf. Sun bathers with cell phones in hand start taking videos or pictures while swimmers get out of the way, seemingly happy to see the majestic animals.

After a good ten minutes, I hear the lifeguard's whistle. Squinting through my sunglasses, I recognize one lifeguard I know—everyone calls him Crockpot, though I'm not sure why.

I wave to him. "Hey, Crockpot."

He runs over to us. "Hey, Dusty. You know the drill. If it was up to me, I could care less all day long about the horses. But you know the snobby rules around here."

"Yes, I know. We weren't gonna stay long. The horses needed a little exercise, but we're going now."

Crockpot looks up at me with his cute, bright-white twenty-something smile. "Hey, when you exit the beach, come past the last guard house. I got some peppermint candies for the horses."

I smile back. "You're the man, Crockpot."

I wave for Gage to follow me, and we make our way to the end of the cove where, conveniently, there is a shower with a hose. Before I can even dismount to wash the sand and salt water off the horses, Gage is down and already on it.

Soon, Crockpot emerges from out of nowhere, holding some candies. Gage gives him a kind look but tells him not too many. I introduce the men as we clean up, and the horses couldn't be happier to receive the sugary treats. I thank Crockpot as we hop back on the horses then take off toward the park trail and head for home.

When we arrive, I realize how late it has gotten and explain to Gage that I have a date.

"A date? With who?" he loudly questions, looking all confused, probably because he has never really heard me mention boyfriends or seen any hanging around. Instead of answering, I just stare at him, embarrassed to tell him I met the guy online. I'm pretty sure Gage is the type of guy that this wouldn't fly well with.

He lifts his cowboy hat up off his brow and cocks his head a little. "Well, who's the lucky man you never mentioned?"

I press my lips together then I blurt it out like vomit. I...I really don't know...him, um, I met him online."

"You did what now?" Gage looks as if he is having trouble holding in a laugh.

"I'm trying an online dating thing...Don't laugh!"

"Oh, darlin', is it that bad around here you have to stoop that low? All those things are just sex hookups. Have you been on one yet, or is the first date?"

"First date," I admit, feeling my face burning in embarrassment.

He puts his hands on his hips. "Okay, where is he taking you?"

"I'm meeting him at O'Hara's Irish Pub."

"All right, do your friends know about this?

"About the date or the online dating in general?"

"Well, now that you ask, all of it."

I fold my arms over my chest. "They are doing it, too, and no, I didn't tell them yet where I'd be."

He lets out a chuckle and shakes his head. "Why do any of you want to get involved in this? Crazy is what it is." He throws his hands up in the air, straightens his hat, and lets out a sigh. "All right. Go." He shoos at me. "Go on and get ready. Let me do my job here."

"Thanks for going on the ride with me, Gage. I had fun." As I walk off, I feel awkward, and I don't really want to leave him.

"Dusty!" he calls out.

I turn back to look at him.

"Please be careful."

"Always am, Gage."

CHAPTER 8

Renee.

"Ice cream!" my girls shout as Nanny Maria helps clear the dinner dishes.

"Okay, I'll take you for ice cream!" I shout back in laughter.

"Can Daddy come, too?"

My heart sinks into my stomach. "I don't think Daddy can come today. He is probably still at work," I sort of lie. Maria gives me a look of disgust.

"Well, do you really want me to get into it with them? They are babies. They don't understand," I tell her.

"What I don't understand is what's going on in that head of yours. Call your doctor, get some meds, and then make it work with your husband. Look, I've been around long enough to know you need help."

I tell the kids to go wait in the other room. As the older one takes the younger by the hand, she says, "Come on. The grownups need to talk."

"Si. You see? They know. They may be babies, but they know. Stop this nonsense, Renee. I hear you at night, crying yourself to sleep."

"I'll be fine," I say sternly.

"Oh. Okay," she says nonchalantly and hands me a framed picture. "I was cleaning and saw this in the spare room. Tell me why you hide your wedding picture if you're fine."

With one look, I burst into tears. "I will be fine," I say through the sobs. "It's going to take time. No one knows what I'm going through; no one understands how I feel. This is my life, not yours."

Maria sits down beside me, grabs my chin, and looks me dead in the face. "Get off the cross; someone else needs the wood."

I return only a stunned gaze—eyes wide, mouth open.

"Stop feeling sorry for yourself. You are not fine. You cry at the sight of this picture. If you were really ready to move on, looking at this photo would not hurt that much. You. Need. Help. My opinion, for what it's worth." She raised both her hands in the air. "Now, come clean yourself up. You need ice cream as much as your babies do."

I do as I'm told, feeling as though I've just gotten a kick in the ass with old-school tough love. I clean my face, touch up my makeup, and off we go.

While I am enjoying my ice cream cone, I get a group text from Dusty.

Renee, Crystal.

Going on date tonight with that Carlos dude. Meeting him in an hour at O'Hara's. That's where we'll be, so keep communication open in case I need help. Bringing mace. Lolol!!

Crystal replies first.

Gotcha. I'm home, working. In court all week. Just say the word!

Then my turn.

Out with my girls already, down the street from there at ice cream parlor. I can send them home with Maria and hang around, if you want.

No worries. I'll let you guys know if I need help. See you both tomorrow night!

As I put my phone away, Dusty's comment gets me thinking about mace. I check my purse to see if mine is still in the little pocket I always keep it in, and it is.

On the way home, I drive slowly past O'Hara's. I spot Dusty's car but decide to wait a couple of hours and just text her to see if she's okay.

* * *

Dusty.

I pull up outside O'Hara's, a typical Irish pub with a juke box blaring today's tunes as well as some older ones. Inside, there are pool tables and lots of harmless local drunks. Heading towards the front the door, I see a nicely dressed gentleman standing, staring at me.

"Anna?" He holds up a tanned hand.

"Yes. Hi, Carlos. Nice to meet you." He escorts me in and directs me over to two empty stools at the end of the bar. I check my surroundings; the restrooms are close by, and there are three bartenders working—two females and one really big dude I believe is the manager and bouncer. I hear someone call him Ron.

O'Hara's is packed tight tonight, both inside and out on the patio. Probably the wonderful weather we had today brought people out.

"What would you like to drink, Anna?"

"I'll take a merlot, please." I smile to be friendly.

"I must say, you are very beautiful, Anna. Your eyes are mysterious. I'm drawn into them. You have me in your spell."

Is he for real with that cheese-ball line? I cock my head at him. "Do I detect a little accent in your speech? Where are you originally from?"

"Yes, my mother is Italian, and my father is from Brazil, where I was born. When I was a kid, we went back and forth then settled here in the States when I was about ten. I have two brothers and two sisters. I am the youngest."

I take a good look at Carlos. His frame is small; he's not a big man at all. Very thin, very tan. He has rings on his fingers and two chain-link bracelets on each wrist. His dark hair is thinning, and he has a hairy chest predictably displaying another gold chain, this one bearing a cross. Very stereotypical. It is hard not to roll my eyes, but I am trying to be nice, be open minded, and have fun, I keep telling myself.

Our small talk goes on and on. He tells me what he does for a living—some kind of marketing. Blah, blah. Boring. He tells me about his divorce and, of course, the ex-wife is a crazy bitch. In my head I'm thinking, *I'd like to hear her side as well.* He has two kids, a boy and girl, of which he shows me pictures. He mentions his mother and how his grandmother is the one who really raised him and his siblings. Honestly, it is all I can do to keep my eyes open. I notice right away he is a heavy drinker. And with each glass of wine he orders, he gets me one, too. They are starting to line up.

I start to feel too much of a buzz. "Hey, do you mind if we order some dinner? I'm hungry, and the wine is going to my head."

He makes a slight frown. "If you are hungry, go ahead and order for yourself. I'm too nervous to eat."

Wow! I thought. *This asshole isn't even buying me a meal.* I look at the bartender to get her attention. When she sees me, I ask her if I could order a burger.

"Sure. And anything for you, sir?"

"No, just another merlot for both of us."

This is going to be an early night for me, but first I've got to eat so I can sober up enough to drive home.

To my unpleasant surprise, Carlos suddenly gets right in my face to talk, leaning in so close to my whole body that my back is pressed up against the wall.

"I want to kiss you now. Is that all right?"

Before I can say no, his lips are on mine and he is forcing his tongue into my mouth. He has wedged one of his legs in between mine, clearly on purpose in order to pin me between the wall, the bar, and him. His hands are everywhere. I finally push at him a little to unlock his mouth from mine. For a little guy, he is stronger than he appears. His eyes, wild and fierce, tell me immediately this jerk-off is just a drunk, and I'm betting a mean one at that. *I have to play this cool and calm, so I don't anger him and cause a scene.*

"What's the matter, Anna? You don't want to kiss me?" he says with his brows furrowed, acting like a spoiled king.

"Well, Carlos," I calmly speak in soft tones, pretending to be shy. "I'm a lady, and I don't like overtly sexual displays of affection in public, and you're a little to handsy. I just met you. What do you say we slow it down a little? Don't you think I deserve that much respect?" *What I deserve is an Oscar for this performance. I just want to get the hell out of here and away from him.*

Weirdly, what pops into my mind is how much fun I had with Gage today and how much of a real gentleman he is.

Finally, my meal arrives. My date looks at my plate, disgust contorting his face.

"Something wrong, Carlos?" I ask him. I want to keep him talking. He is starting to get slightly off balance and speak with an increasingly forceful tone.

"Why you eat that in front of me? Greasy meat—it's not good for your body. With me, I will put you on strict diet. You will stay healthy. And you won't eat this." He grabs at the onion slice and tosses it onto the bar.

"What do you have against onions?" I ask, keeping my cool.

"No eating onions tonight." He slams his hand down on the bar. "I'm going to spend the night wrapped around your body, and I don't want any part of you tasting like an onion."

I laugh. But he is not laughing back. His eyes darken.

"You think I'm funny now?"

I bite into my burger, and with a mouthful I reply, "Yes, I kind of do."

He waits for me to swallow my bite then grabs my face in both his hands. "Does it look like I'm joking?" He wraps me in a very strong embrace and assaults my mouth with his. I push him off with more force this time. I am still trying to act calm, so I tell him, "Slow it down, please. We're in public."

Again, he slams his hand down on the bar. "I don't care, and I don't care what they think," he booms with an underlying growl while his tanned face reddens and his eyes blaze beneath deeply furrowed brows.

This asshole must have had a few drinks before I got here. He is way past a buzz.

"I care," I answer firmly. "I don't want to be fondled in front of a bar full of people like some piece of meat. And I don't appreciate the attitude. Why don't you have some water."

Having lost my appetite, I set my burger back onto the plate. Since I don't want to agitate him any further, I am outwardly remaining very calm. Unbelievably, he again closes in on me, forcing his mouth onto mine. This time I push hard against his chest to get him to back off, but I can't budge him. It's pissing me off that he is strangely strong for such a petite guy.

While his assault is going on, I think about excusing myself to go to the restroom, where I will call one of the girls. Even if I could get past him now to get to my car, I figure there is a good chance he would follow me home.

When his mouth finally unlocks from mine, he has a strange look on his face. Confused at first, I suddenly realize the reason for the odd look: there, holding Carlos by the skin of his neck, is Gage, all lean muscle and cowboy hat towering over Carlos by a whole eight inches.

"Dusty, what's going on here?" Gage says in deep, direct tones.

"Put me down, you redneck asshole," Carlos slurs.

Gage lets go, and Carlos drops like a lead balloon.

"Now, I don't know who taught you how to treat a lady, but from where I was sittin', I heard her tell you she didn't like it and to slow down."

Gage's baritone voice seems to shake everything in a five-foot radius and hits Carlos right in the face before Ron, the manager, steps up and asks Gage if he needs any help taking out the trash.

Carlos gets to his feet and grabs me by the arm. "Mind your own business, dick head!" he tells Gage. "Come on, Anna." He tugs me harder.

"I'm not going anywhere with you. I suggest you leave!"

"No!" he spurts continuing to slur. "Not leaving here without you. We are on a date, and I'm spending my night with you."

By this time, his eyes aren't even focusing properly. But, before I can say anything else, Gage tosses Ron a glance and Ron nods once. Gage hits Carlos with one punch to the face; I hear a crack as it knocks him out cold. I'm speechless, watching it all unfold like a movie.

Gage gently puts his hand on my shoulder. "You okay, Dusty?"

Wide-eyed and in awe, I just nod.

"Okay. I'll be right back. Stay here. Don't move." He turns to Ron.

"I got my eye on her, Gage. Go ahead."

"Thanks, man. I'll get this shit out of your bar."

"Great. I'll have a cold one waiting here for ya."

Gage picks Carlos up off the floor and hauls him outside, the customers clearing a path before him as if he is Moses parting the sea. I sit back and push my plate away, telling myself not to throw up.

One of the female bartenders hands me a glass of cold water. "Here—drink this," she says with a smile. "That asshole comes in here once a week and gets polluted. He meets women all the time. You would be surprised at the desperate ones who actually go home with him. They probably don't realize he's an abusive drunk or maybe just fall for his lines, but I was watching you." She continues, "You had him pegged from the beginning. The scary thing is I could tell he was really into you. I never saw him get that physical before. You were smart trying to keep him calm. He is a nasty drunk. Good thing Gage got here and saw you."

"You know Gage?" I ask with a shaky voice.

"Yeah, he's been here a few times. Usually alone. He's always been nice and pleasant."

I start to feel strange and my legs begin to shake. The bartender notices. "Oh, I think you're having a panic attack, sweetie."

"Is that what this is? I feel all shaky and tight in my chest."

When Gage returns, the bartender tells him of my current situation.

"Dusty, you all right?" Gage asks with concern.

I turn to him, but all I can do is breathe deeply.

"Jesus, you're shaking. Come on—I'm taking you home."

With Gage's help, I walk out of O'Hara's. Ron is at the door with a big smile on his face, looking almost giddy. He gives Gage a high five. "Man, I took a picture with my phone. You got to show me how you did that."

I glance at Gage, wondering what they are talking about. Ron notices the expression on my face and looks at me with sympathy. I guess I don't look so good, because he holds my hand for a minute and says, "You come back any time, Dusty. That asshole won't be allowed in here anymore, I promise you."

I feel Gage's arm wrap around my waist. "Yeah, thanks Ron. Let me get her home. I think she's in a little bit of shock."

As we walk through the parking lot over to Gage's truck, I point at my car as we pass by it.

"No, no, no...I'll get your car tomorrow. You ride home with me tonight." He helps me climb in, and he buckles me up, my body shivering as he touches me. "It's fine, now. Relax. Breathe," he whispers.

He starts his truck and just stares at me for a few moments. I look back at him. I can't get my voice out, so I mouth the words thank you. He smiles. "No worries. I saw you were in trouble."

I put my hands up and motion around, finally managing to croak the words, "Where did he go? What did you do?"

Gage smiles and puts the truck in gear, drives through the back of the lot, and points to a dumpster. There's Carlos, all tied up with rope like a hog.

As we drive home, thoughts of that sledgehammer rapist enter my mind. "Oh my God," I say aloud, jolting Gage just a little.

"What? What's the matter?" he shouts.

"I just thought about the rapist! What if Carlos is the rapist?"

Gage chuckles. "Not even close. This guy gets too drunk. I have seen him plenty of times in that bar. Which brings me to my next question. What in the hell were you thinking going on a date with that dude? What— nothing better on that dating site but him?"

I look at Gage as little stress tears well up in my eyes.

"Oh shit, I'm sorry. Don't cry. Shit. My bad. I'm sorry. Okay...none of my business."

Oddly, I start to laugh at the uncomfortable way tears make him react. "What's the matter, tough guy? Can't handle a few tears?"

"That would be a no. Especially from a woman I'm fond of. It's my kryptonite. Makes me weak in the knees"

I roar with laughter, but Gage just looks at the road with a smirk.

"I amuse you now. I show you my sensitive side, and you laugh. All right, I see how it is."

"Thank you, Gage. I know what you're doing. Thank you. I'm feeling better."

Awkward silence fills the truck as we arrive home. I can't help myself and put my hand on his shoulder.

"Gage, you're fond of me?"

He takes off his hat and tosses it on the dashboard in a little frustrated motion. "Well, hell yeah, I'm fond of you. You are the whole package. You're a businesswoman, you cook, you love football, you ride horses, you're kind, and you're beautiful, inside and out."

Gage has no idea how much I need to hear this.

"Gage, don't leave me tonight. I just need to have you near."

In response, he helps me to the front door and unlocks it. As we walk in, I tell him I need a hot shower. "I want to wash this night and the smell of Carlos off of me."

"I'll be right out here, watchin' the tube," he answers softly.

Even though Carlos is not a crazy rapist, he was definitely out of control. I felt violated by his disgusting kisses and his body pinning mine.

As the soothing water pours over my body, I let my tears fall and mix with it, purging out all the trauma of the experience.

When I am finished and dried off, I put on a night shirt and go to find Gage. In the living room, he has the T.V. on, just as he said he would. I sit down and cuddle up next to him. As he puts his arm around me, we give each other a look, but that's all. Gage doesn't try to kiss me or anything. He lets me just be comforted, and that's all I need.

I guess hours passed and I had fallen asleep, because the next thing I know, Gage is waking me to go to bed. Before I can get my feet on the floor, though, I suddenly feel myself being lifted off the couch. Gage carries me to my room, gently places me on the bed, and covers me with my soft down comforter. He turns to walk away, but I reach for him.

"I'll just be on the couch," he says.

"What, are we twelve? Come to bed, Gage," I urge. "Just to sleep. I just need to touch you and know you're here."

He takes off his clothes but leaves his underwear in place and climbs in bed with me. He kisses my head and brings his body against mine in a spooning position yet never touches me sexually at all. We soon fall into a peaceful sleep, lying in each other's embrace all night.

CHAPTER 9

Crystal.

"Hello. Good morning, Crystal. How are you?"

I love Henry's enthusiasm, and we haven't even met yet.

"Good morning." I steal a quick glance at the clock. Nine a.m., here, which means it's a super-early a.m. in his time zone. "Jesus, Henry, isn't it, like, the middle of the night there?"

"Yes. What can I say? You were on my mind. I know you doubled up on your workload. How's it going?"

"I'm prepared for two court dates and one mediation. And that's if everyone keeps up their end of the bargain. You know it's always the same shit, deadbeat dads or wives fighting prenuptials. I see it all the time. Makes me grow leery and sad because of what humans do to one another. At some point people do fall in love, but somehow we have a way of screwing it up."

"Indeed, but have faith. Some people fall in love and stay that way. My parents are going on fifty-one years."

"Wow! God bless them. What's their secret?"

"Dad says you have to keep your lady happy. If she's happy, everyone is happy." He laughs, and it's intoxicating. I'm craving to hear it in person.

"I think that's very smart and sound advice, Henry."

"Okay, baby, I'm going to get some more sleep before I start my day, and may I say, I'm looking forward to being there next weekend. Got anything in mind for us?"

"As a matter of fact, I do. How does a nice ride out on my boat sound? We can go to so many restaurants by way of water then just drop anchor off the shore line. We can talk, get to know each other."

"That sounds perfect. I like the way you think. I'll call you later."

***

Renee.

"Are you serious? Gage knocked him out?!"

"Yeah, you should have seen it. The whole thing more than startled me. I was completely shaken up. But Gage took care of me. It was so…so…charming? Does anyone ever say that anymore? Chivalrous, I suppose."

"Oh my God. How scary! So…are you guys a thing now?"

"Ummm…yeah, I think we are. When I woke up this morning, he brought me a coffee then went on his way to do his work. He gave me another kiss on my forehead."

"Okay, I'm thinking girls' night real soon, maybe sooner than Friday," I suggest to Dusty.

"Yes. Agreed. I'll call Crystal. I'm sure she'll need a break before Friday. She's doing double time so she can have next weekend with this Henry guy…which sounds promising, I have to say.

* * *

Dusty.

Looking at my calendar book, I see a few appointments I need to attend to this week. I know Crystal is swamped, so from what I'm guessing, girls' night will have to be Thursday. I call Renee back to fill her in. *Now*, I decide, *I'd better get dressed and get this day started.*

As I make my way out of the house, Gage approaches on my horse Miguel. I smile up at him while shielding my eyes from the sun. "I'm off. I'll be home around six."

"Have a good day, my lady," he says, and I swoon. "Hey...uh..."—he hesitates—"can I...umm...or would you come to...Can I take you out tonight, you know, properly?"

"Sure," I say, wearing a dopey smirk. "On a date?"

"Of course on a date." He sighs. "Why do you torture me?"

"Because it's fun," I tell him as I jump into my car. I start the ignition, put her in drive, and roll out the driveway. A quick glance in the rearview mirror confirms he is still there, watching me leave.

***

Renee.

It has been a very long week with the kids' activities and trying hard not to feel so sad all the time. It's draining me. I did, however, talk with G.W. a few times, and we are planning our rendezvous. He seems very sweet and wants me to feel comfortable with him before our blind date.

Tonight I want to have a little fun, so I've managed to pull together something amusing for tonight's girls' night in. I invited a few more friends and called our local adult store, Adam & Eve, and scheduled a Secret Party. I had to call Frank to take the girls for the evening as my nanny, Maria, wanted to attend the festivities, too.

The woman who is here to instruct the partygoers is a beautiful blonde with a short pixie haircut. She seems to be about ten years older than I, and for the life of me, I can't stop looking at her big, fake boobs. Honestly, they are frigging perfect! She introduces herself as Gina as she comes in toting a trunk of sexual toys and goodies. Soon, she starts to pull them out and display them on my coffee table and on a little fold-out table she's brought. She asks if it would be all right for her to put Bob on my dining room table as a centerpiece.

"Who is Bob?" I ask, totally confused.

"This is BOB!" she says as she gently places an object in my hands.

My eyes grow wide; my face gets warm. "That's the biggest, brightest-blue dildo I have ever seen in my life!" I shriek.

"That there is Big Boy Bob," she begins her repertoire. "Battery Operated Boyfriend, hence B-O-B. He's blue, he has balls, he has a suction cup under him to make him secure, even in the shower. His girth is two-and-a-half inches, and he is twelve inches long. He vibrates through the whole shaft and he moves...in a circle." She snaps her fingers and winks.

"Jesus Christ! Is that for show? Or for use?" I inquire.

Gina eyes me calmly. "You can use it," she says, smirking.

"Ouch! On who?" I ask in shock as my mind races. In my wildest dreams, I couldn't imagine a penis that large. "Does that...can that fit in there?" I ask incredulously, pointing to my lady parts.

"Oh, it'll fit, sweetie," she says, still wearing an evil but playful smirk.

The doorbell rings, and Dusty lets herself in. "Hello!" she calls out. As I turn towards her, she sees me standing there with BOB in my hands. "Renee, hon, what the hell is that?"

Before I can open my mouth, Gina steps towards Dusty and extends her hand.

"Hi there! My name's Gina, and I'm your Secret Party host for the evening, and that right there is the star of the show, BOB."

Dusty's face turns the same shade of red as mine must be. Her eyes are as wide as mine, too. Her lips start to quiver, holding in a laugh. "Renee, why don't you put BOB down and pour us some wine?"

I circle around to my dining-room table, move some trays of food out of the way, and securely stick BOB smack in the middle. Both Gina and Dusty come up on either side of me. We stare at BOB in all its glory, marveling at the specks of light cast by my chandelier and glinting off BOB's shiny, blue head.

Dusty gestures with her hand. "It makes me want to stand and salute it!"

Instantly, BOB starts to vibrate and move in a mechanical, hypnotic circle that mesmerizes us even more. Gina smiles at us, showing us BOB's remote in her hand.

"Holy shit!" I exclaim, cocking my head to one side.

Dusty walks around to the other side of the table and swallows hard. Pulling out her phone, she snaps a picture. I glance up at her in awe. She takes a deep breath. "Crystal said she might be a little late, but I'm sending her this picture, telling her to try not to keep BOB waiting."

After the lightheadedness leaves us, we come down with a serious case of giggles. The doorbell keeps ringing, and one by one, our friends are introduced to BOB. It all sounds like, "Hi! Glad you could make it. Would you like to meet BOB?"

When Crystal finally arrives, we end up as a nice even group of eight. She marches right in the door and appears to be slightly out of breath. She slams the door behind her and yells, "Where the fuck is BOB?!" We all point towards the dining-room table.

"Hello, Big Boy. Where have you been all my life?" she coos.

We go hysterical with laughter. "Oh my God! I need a glass of wine!" Crystal shouts.

"I got you, girlfriend. Come on in here. Leave BOB alone for a minute. I don't think he's going anywhere."

Crystal, very giddy, skips into the kitchen. I hand her a glass of merlot. Her smile is big;

her eyes are wide. "Whose idea was it to have a Secret Party?"

I raise my hand. "That would be me."

"Oh...my...God. I so needed this perversion diversion. What made you think of the idea?"

I giggle. "The other day, I felt I needed—we all needed—something fun and uninhibited."

Dusty walks up, holding something called *Hot Gel*. "Well, I for one think it's a great idea."

"I couldn't agree more," Crystal replies. "I need to blow off some steam after the week I had. And in seven days, ladies, Henry is flying in!"

Suddenly, Gina pipes in, "Well, then, you're going to want some goodies for your weekend. Gather 'round, ladies, and let's get your freak on!"

For a good hour, Gina goes through a mix of sexual toys that I'll admit I never even knew existed. We laugh so much we cry. Around ten, Gina packs up her playthings and tells us she has another party tomorrow and it is going to be all gay-male couples. That's one party I would definitely pee my pants at—I would giggle so much! I can only imagine how fun those guys would be!

I sit down on the couch with my two best friends. Now that everyone else has gone, the three of us decide to hang out and catch up.

After Dusty fills us in on her little bar-fight episode, she raises her wine glass. "Good party. Great idea, Renee! I haven't laughed so hard in a long time."

"Here, heeere!" Crystal chimes in. "Oh man, that was fun, and did I hear her say she has another party over at the old-folks' home next week?"

"Yes. How messed up is that?" I answer.

"That must be a fun job to do, huh?" Dusty asks. "I guess you can't be shy about much."

"She makes it fun. Also, did you notice she pushes personal safety and safe sex?" Crystal added.

"Yeah, you would certainly need to practice safety with that sex-swing-chair thingy!"

Dusty let out a laugh. "Right! It looks kind of dangerous."

"So, Crystal, Henry is coming to meet you. Are you nervous? Excited?" I ask as I am so excited for her.

She sits upright from her slouching position on the sofa and puts her glass down on the coffee table. "You know what? I am nervous but not in a bad way or the way you think I might be. I'm nervous about the fact I've never met this man in person. We talk on the phone all the time and about so much, and I know that's not the same thing. But I'm not afraid to meet him. I honestly feel like I know him. That's what is making me nervous. It's too premature to say I have these feelings, but my gut is saying he's the one. How is that possible? That's what's scary."

Dusty sits up next. "No, I kind of get it. Gage has been working at my ranch now for, what, all of a couple months? And though I hate to admit it, I think for both of us, from the time we first met, there was a connection of some sort. We finally went on a proper date—dinner, nothing more—and honestly, we haven't even kissed yet, but I can't picture my life without him. That truly is crazy."

"You haven't kissed yet?!" I shriek. "What in the hell are you waiting for?"

"Really, Dusty," Crystal chimes in, in agreement. "The man hog-tied some drunk asshole for you. You know what you've got to do? Go home and kiss your hero!"

We all laugh.

Dusty takes a sip of her wine. "You're probably right, but Gage seems like an old soul or old fashioned. You know, like such a gentleman he was gonna sleep on the couch, for God's sake."

"I can't believe he didn't touch you all night. That's got to take some restraint," I say.

"Maybe he's waiting for me to give him a signal? Or make the first move?"

Crystal sits back and puts her feet up. "Dusty, honey, when you get home, just kiss the man."

"Agreed." I raise my hand.

"Now on to you," Crystal says in her lawyer voice. "What are you doing about Frank?"

"Nothing. We're separated. I'm still dating. In fact, I have been talking to someone online."

"The G.W. guy you told me about?" Dusty asks.

"G.W.?" Crystal questions. "His name is initials? And not even normal ones like B.J. or T.J. What does it stand for? Gee Whiz?" she giggles.

"I'm not sure," I admit. "He seems very nice. We've been talking almost daily, first online then on the phone."

"Are you going to meet him?" Dusty asks.

"Yes, but like you mentioned with Gage, he seems like he wants to get to know me better first, maybe so we don't feel uncomfortable when we do meet. I think it's good. We are slowly getting to know more about each other."

"Okay, then. Seems like you've got it under control," Crystal says. "Now, more importantly, who bought stuff tonight?"

Dusty's hand goes up. "I bought some lotions and that Hot Gel kit."

Crystal nods. "I did, too. You know, years ago I was with this man for a short time. His name was Danny. Well, he was a bit older and sometimes he couldn't rise to the occasion, sexually, so I bought him a penis pump. Frigging thing cost me three hundred dollars.

"So, I'm at the adult store, and they teach me how to use it. Then the sales girl hands me these little rubber-band things. Okay, they tell me, once I get him all pumped up, I've got to place the band around the base of his dick and under his balls to keep the blood flow in there and secure.

"Well, I go home and I'm so excited because I'm gonna fix Mr. Softie. I show him what I bought and how it works, and it's supposed to be fun and nothing short of a miracle. Now, you've got to picture this guy. He was a big, burly dude, ex-police, ex-military, six feet tall with broad shoulders. He was probably so embarrassed that he couldn't get it up; not even the pills helped him. But you know me, I didn't sweat it too much, plus he was so talented at going down on me that my vajayjay literally craved him. Seriously, I could've sat on his face all day! Anyway, every night I would lube him up, put this contraption on him, and start pumping. His dick would get engorged and almost turn purple! His penis would grow up that tube. I'd get so far then he would raise a hand and say, 'Stop!' because it got a little painful for him.

"Well, one night, I guess I used a little too much lube. My hands were slick with the stuff. So, after I pumped him up to where he should be, I grabbed one of those rubber-band thingies and started to place one around the base of his dick and underneath those old balls of his and make sure all my pumping kept him from shriveling. Well, the rubber band slips from my greasy fingers and snaps him in the balls! He sprang from the bed and let out a howl as he tried to pry that pump right off himself, but of course it wasn't budging, and the more he tried to pull it off, the more it was stuck and causing him pain."

As we all bawl with laughter, I finally manage to squeal out the words, "What did you do?"

Crystal calms herself down enough from laughing to speak. "I was on the floor laughing, and of course he did not think anything about it was funny, which made me laugh harder! I asked him how he could keep a straight face. But he didn't think that was funny either! And that was the end of the penis pump." She claps her hands as to wipe the thought away. "When he finally got it off, he tossed it back in the bag, shoved it in the closet, and I never saw it again."

"Do you still have it?" Dusty asks through teary-eyed laughter.

"No, when we broke up, that son of a bitch took it with him!"

We roar even harder with laughter.

It takes a few minutes for us to calm ourselves down. "I'm getting a headache from laughing so hard," I say, holding my head. I look at my friends. They have black tear smudges at the outer corners of their eyes, and I'm sure I do, too.

"So...did anyone buy BOB?" Crystal inquires. We are silent, at first, then I sheepishly raise my hand.

"Oh my God, Renee! You didn't! When it comes in, let us know how it works for ya!" Dusty says.

Crystal motions with her wine glass "It will probably take a few weeks to come in, right?"

"Uh, no. Actually, I told Gina to sell me that one!" I point at my dining room table, where BOB is still standing, shining like a big, blue trophy.

CHAPTER 10

Renee.

I'm awakened by the ringing of my cell phone. I roll over and eye the time: six a.m. I reach for my cell, and it's G.W. Surprised, I answer it.

"Hello?"

"Good morning, Anna. Hon, sorry to call so early, but I was thinking about you all night."

Confused, I ask, "You were?"

"Well, of course I was. Why does that shock you? Didn't anyone ever tell you that before?"

"Yes, I guess so, but we haven't even met yet."

"Well, that's why I'm calling you so early. Why don't we fix that, like say, today? Why don't we meet somewhere nice, in public for a coffee? No pressure."

"Okay, sure. Where?"

"I'm a little out of the general area today. I'm stayin' in a Hampton Inn over in Hollywood. I'm working on a construction job, but I'm not expecting you to come to the hotel. Like I said, we can meet at a diner or the Dunkin Donuts—whatever. I have the afternoon off, so I can buy you lunch, brunch, anything you want."

"You want me to drive over to Hollywood?"

"If you don't mind. See, that's just part of my job, and I stay over because we start work early in the morning and I don't want to commute. Please say you'll come and meet me. I work till noon today, so I have some free time."

"Sure. Why not? Text me an address of a local diner, and I'll meet you there at one p.m."

"Thanks, buddy. I promise I'll be a perfect gentleman."

* * *

I hang up and think, *How strange. Unexpectedly he wants to meet, but we have been talking for a couple of weeks now. Just have a little fun, I tell myself. It's broad daylight and in public. I will tell the girls, though, what I'm doing. How cute that he called me buddy. I like it.*

As I make my way to the kitchen to get my morning coffee, my thoughts are with Crystal. Henry is coming in for the weekend, and I smile at the thought of her happiness.

***

Crystal.

"How was the flight?" I ask Henry on the phone.

"Wonderful—we landed," he jokes. "I am en route to your condo. I rented a car, and navigation says you're about twenty minutes from the airport."

"Yes, that sounds about right. I'll see you soon. Call me if you can't find it."

Within twenty minutes, my doorman lets Henry up. I open the door, and I'm stunned by his presence. Even though we've FaceTimed a few times, he just seems to be more magnificent in person. He enters and drops one small suitcase down, searches my face, and pulls me into him but hesitates to kiss me. He simply stares into my eyes then, after a few beats, gently brushes his lips to mine. I instinctively wrap my arms around him and deepen the kiss.

"Now, that is a warm welcome." He speaks so smoothly that it comforts my very being. I relax, my eyes gazing upon him.

"I was so nervous, but now that you're here...and that kiss...I'm fine, like I've always known you."

"Kindred spirits, I suppose," he suggests with a warm, assuring smile.

I show him around the condominium then point out the view from my living-room window. "We have dinner reservations tonight at a wonderful bistro at seven. But for now, I have a light lunch set out for us on the veranda. Go and get out of that suit and get comfy."

* * *

Dusty.

"You girls were right. I got home the other night, walked right up to Gage, and kissed him hard. He picked me up and tossed me on the bed as if I was a rag doll."

"Okay. And..." Renee purrs.

"And, he looks me dead in my face, tells me it's been far too long for him, and not to be disrespectful, but he might lose control and fuck my brains out and doesn't want to hurt me."

"Holy shit!"

"That's what I said! And out loud, too. Then I politely asked him to please fuck my brains out. Renee, he was so hard and so intense, I had three orgasms. We could not get enough of each other. We did it almost all night long."

"Oh God, Dusty. How jealous am I? I need a good, rough toss on the bed."

I laugh at her comment. "Everyone needs that, Renee. So, are you going over to meet G.W.?"

"Yeah, I figure, why not? He seems very nice, but we'll just have to wait and see. I may not be into him."

"True. And be careful. Text me the time and place, and let me know you're okay and when you're on your way home. If you need me, just say the word."

"You got it. Thanks."

"How do you think Crystal's doing with Henry? I wish I were a fly on the wall over there," I say with a giggle.

"I was thinking that this morning, also. I can't wait to hear all about it."

Renee.

G.W. sends a text telling me to meet him at a seafood place called Juniper's.

It's a cute place, not too fancy, and it is on the Intracoastal Waterway. As I pull up and park, I see this average-looking man waving at me. In my reply text to him, I had told G.W. I would be driving a white Cadillac Escalade, so I guess he kept a lookout.

He approaches me and appears to be just an inch or two taller than I am. Kind of on the skinny side and very tan, with sandy-colored hair that looks a little like a Brillo pad. Clean-shaven and smelling of Polo cologne, he is dressed very nicely. "Hey," he says and offers a hug, so I comply.

We enter the restaurant and sit at a table outside, overlooking the water. He pulls out the chair for me; I sit down and take in the view.

"Wow, I've never been here before. What a charming little place."

"I thought you'd like it. I spotted it on my way to work and thought it'd be good food, and public, but not too crowded so we can talk."

"You're really concerned about making sure we are in public, aren't you?"

"I'm just making sure you feel safe. You know how these dating websites can be. You never know who you might meet. Better safe than sorry."

As he mentions that, I decide to come clean about my real name, now, but I won't tell him too much more. "By the way, you can call me Renee. I use Anna for the dating website only, just to be safe."

"Ah, the old fake-name game." He chuckles. "Anything else you'd like to come clean about?"

"Umm...no, not yet, or not today." I laugh. He just sits with a smirk, which is endearing in a way but also puts me off a little bit. I am so nervous, and he senses it.

"Tell you what, Renaaay..." He draws out my name with sarcasm in his voice but smiles. "Let's get some wine or a cocktail of your choice and you can relax a little. No pressure and no more lies. How we gonna get to know each other if we lie?"

As lunch goes on, we talk mostly about me. Never letting my guard down, I'm careful to not tell him where I live or my kids' names, who my friends are, who my husband is or what he does. I don't even tell him my last name, though he keeps pushing for me to open up. But when I ask the same of him, he also isn't forthcoming with information. I only discover he is divorced from a bitch, has no kids, and no family other than his mom. He works freelance on construction jobs all over Florida.

Our conversation stays light: What foods do you like? What are your favorite movies? Are you allergic to anything? What favorite trips have you been on? It all seems very innocent but very cautious. I probably wouldn't have been so apprehensive about telling him stuff if he were more open himself.

After a few hours and some awkward silences, I'm thinking maybe this isn't working. We've had only an average conversation, nothing to get excited about, and I suddenly just want to go home. So, I use my kids as an excuse.

"Wow, look at the time. It's going to take me a good thirty to forty minutes to get back, and I like to be home for my girls. This was lovely. Please give me a call when your job is finished, and we'll get together again."

As soon as I heard myself say it, I thought, *Ugh, you're boring and a little weird. Shut up. Just stop talking.*

He stands. "Let me walk you to your car?"

"Sure, why not?"

"And may I hold your hand?" he asks.

I nod. He gently takes it. His palm is rough from working with his hands. When I get to my car, I quickly open the door. Without warning, he slams it shut.

"Not without a kiss goodbye, buddy."

With force, he spins me into him and gives me a hard, powerful kiss. At first I don't like it, but then I just go with it. His hands grip my arms like a vice. For a wiry guy, he's sort of strong. He breaks the kiss and winks at me.

"Sorry if I was too forward, but I've kind of been waiting to do that for hours." He laughs.

I laugh back, but I'm still put off. I don't like that I can't read this guy. I wonder if he's just another fuck boy like Steve.

G.W. returns to being a gentleman, opening my car door and helping me in. "Be safe driving back home. I'll call you in a day or two, Renaaay..." A throaty, raspy chuckle comes out of him, and it's just a touch creepy.

"Great," I say, starting up the car. I watch him walk away before I text Dusty and tell her I'm fine, I'm on my way home, and the date was strange.

She texts back:

Strange how?

***

Crystal.

"Here, give me your key."

I hand Henry the key to my door. He unlocks it and enters first. I follow behind and tap the light switch.

"Would you like a drink?" I ask.

"Sure. Do you have any brandy?"

"Coming up." I pour some into two tumblers and hold one out to him. "Let's go sit on the veranda." He follows me out, and we collapse on two lounge chairs, side by side.

"Dinner was fantastic," he says. "What a great little place."

"I'm glad you liked it. It's one of my favorites."

He motions with his hand. "This view is great, Crystal. Did you seek out the place, or did you get lucky?"

I take a sip of the amber liquid, and it soothes my throat. "A little of both, I think. After my divorce, I kept my eye on three different places that all had one thing in common." I point with the glass of brandy in my fingertips. "The ocean. They were all on the beach, facing the Atlantic. The view from my office is the same. I figure if I'm going to live by the water, then I might as well be able to look at it. Keeps me calm, I think."

Henry sits up and finishes off the rest of the liquor in his glass. He moves my legs over and joins me on my lounger. He's staring right into my eyes. I smile.

"You are beautiful, Crystal. I want to learn more about you, get to know you, every inch of you. I couldn't wait to touch you, to kiss you."

My eyes pierce into his. "Kiss me now." He does. "Touch me now." His hands gently caress my back and down my hips to my thighs, where he gently pulls them apart, hiking up my sundress. Wet kisses touch my belly then my legs, and then he teases my slit with swipes of his tongue. My back arches in response, and he slides his palms under my ass, lifting me enough to get a better taste.

Suddenly, he picks me up and carries me to the bedroom.

***

Dusty.

"What do you mean the date was strange?"

I wait for Renee to respond. She's chewing gum and snapping it. I know she does this when she's anxious.

"Well..." she says and looks up at the ceiling. "He was intense...you know...really watching me, as if he was studying me. And there were all these awkward pauses between questions. I noticed he was not forthcoming with information, so I didn't give him any on me either. We kept the conversation light. All our talks on the phone seemed as if we had more of a connection. But being with him, I felt like I was on display."

I listen carefully to Renee as she chomps her gum with force. "Okay. So, it was an awkward first meeting. Do you think you're still into him?"

"Weirdly, I am," she states, looking like she is shocked by her own answer. "He wants to see me again, and I think I want to go. This is becoming intriguing, like he's a mystery."

"Yes, or maybe you are to him. You played the game. You went hit for hit with him on yes-and-no questions. He didn't go deep, so you didn't. I'm sure he was waiting for an open door."

"You're probably right. Okay. Cool. I feel better. He wants to go out this Friday night; I'll tell him yes," she says, bobbing her head.

"Don't forget to tell us where, and keep your cell charged."

Renee takes the gum from her mouth and wraps it in one of the cocktail napkins I placed on the table earlier when I poured us some wine. "So..." she says softly. "How's Gage?"

"Gage is doing just fine." I feel my face flush.

"Oh my God, Dusty. You're blushing!"

"I know! How insane is that? Like I'm seventeen again and just lost my virginity. I must admit, I'm loving this. It even feels so much better than when I was with Kenny in the beginning. I feel a vibe with Gage. I really think there is something special. It's unusual for me to say this so soon, but it's like somehow the universe put us together in some beautiful accident."

"Wow, Dusty! I don't think I've ever heard you say anything so positive about any guy."

I glance at Renee and realize she might be right. "I think it's all about to change."

"I'll drink to that," Renee says, holding up her glass of pinot grigio. I follow with my glass, and we clink to new beginnings.

***

Crystal.

The light of day comes streaming into my bedroom. Slowly, I begin to awaken along with my body, which doesn't seem like mine. I feel as though I've done a wild workout. My muscles are sore, especially in my legs. I smile, remembering the night. I believe I've just had the best sex of my life. I peek over at Henry.

He's awake, too, and peeking back.

"Good morning, beautiful." His voice, rugged with morning, is still so velvety.

I smile at him. "How does coffee sound?"

"It sounds wonderful." He snuggles in closer to me and like a bear, engulfs me in his arms. He gives me a quick kiss, rolls me gently off the bed, and helps me to my feet while delicately holding my hand.

"Okay, Fred Astaire, I'll go make us that coffee."

He follows me to the kitchen and takes a seat on the stool at the counter. "So, do you dance?" he asks.

"I can. I'm no ballroom dancer, but I've got rhythm."

"With those long legs of yours, you must ballroom dance with me. I will teach you." His smile is devilishly playful.

"Okay, I made us a pot instead of the k-cups. I figured we would need the whole pot. Let's give it a few minutes."

He cocks an eyebrow at me, "I know something we can do in the meantime."

"Oh? What's that?" I ask, turning around.

There stands Henry in his grey boxer briefs with a boner so hard and long it looks painful. "Come"—he lifts his hand to me—"come shower with me."

I gasp.

***

Renee.

G.W. is blowing up my phone. I feel awkward but answer anyway. "Hi," I say softly into the phone.

153

"Hey, buddy. I'm checkin' to see if we can go out Friday night."

I take a deep breath. "Yeah, sure. Where are we going?"

"Well, I thought it'd be nice to meet at Lunar Park for a picnic then go for a walk on the beach. It's going to be a full moon and a nice evening."

I quickly assess Lunar Park in my head. It's close to home, close to Dusty's ranch. "Okay, that sounds lovely. I can meet you there."

"Great. I was thinking around seven."

"That works for me."

"Hey, Renee, I'm sorry about our lunch date the other day. I want to apologize. I was really nervous, and I think I came off as creepy."

I laugh. "You know what, G.W.? You kind of did, but I'll forgive you."

"Thanks, buddy. I'll be better this time. I promise."

"See you Friday," I say with laughter echoing in my voice. I'm feeling much better about things now.

***

Crystal.

"While making love to you all day in bed sounds perfect, I assume you have something else planned for us today?"

I roll off the bed and smile at Henry's question. "I do. I'm taking you out on my boat. It's a perfect day for it."

I open the blinds as Henry gets out of bed and walks up behind me, and we both take in the view of the ocean. The sea is calm and smooth as glass with the bright mid-morning sun reflecting off of it like gold glitter. "The weather today is fantastic for cruising on the boat—seventy-eight degrees with very low humidity and a pleasant, light breeze. I'll pack us up a lunch and two bottles of wine."

Henry's smile is the only answer I need. We get dressed and packed, and within a half hour, we are on board, pushing off the dock as I maneuver the boat.

Henry comes to stand next to me. "Will you let me have a go at the driver's seat once we get out in open water?"

"Sure. This boat is a dream to navigate."

"A Sea Ray?"

"Yes, SDX 270 outboard."

"Twenty-five?"

"Twenty-seven foot."

"It's beautiful. You handle it well."

"Here you go. We're out. I'll direct you to the perfect spot to drop anchor."

Minutes later, we arrive at the inlet. It's a busy Saturday afternoon, and I advise Henry to go a little farther away from the clutter of boaters, where people are fishing and swimming. I tend to stay clear of all that. He handles the boat nicely, and we drop anchor.

I take off my sundress to reveal a sexy black bikini. We help each other lather up with sun lotion, and Henry pours us some wine. He hands me a glass of pinot and raises his glass in the air.

"To a beautiful weekend, a beautiful day, and a beautiful woman."

We clink our glasses. "Thank you, Henry. I feel the same way."

***

Dusty.

"Hey, lady. What ya up to?"

I look up from my laptop to see Gage standing in the doorway of my study. The sleeves of his aqua-blue western button-down shirt, smudged with dirt from working my ranch, are rolled up just enough to show muscular forearms. And the sheen of perspiration at the base of his throat nearly glistens on his tanned skin. Such a beautiful sight.

"Well, at the local club I belong to, there is a benefit tonight called Denim and Diamonds. All the local businesses donate their services, and profits go to disabled children. I offer spa services to their moms, and I help fund horseback riding for the kids at the local therapeutic riding facility, or sometimes I just have them come over here for a visit with my horses. Some kids don't get out much because of their disabilities. Anyway, I wasn't planning to attend this year, but we do have a table waiting for us. I can give Renee a call; she will probably come. Crystal has company this weekend. Otherwise, she would be there, too. But I really would love it if you would come with me."

Gage removes his cowboy hat from his head and shyly gives me a smile. "Well, my lady, nothing would make me happier than to escort you to this function. Now, I have the denim, but I don't have diamonds." He laughs, and I smile up at him.

"That's fine. The diamonds are supposed to be my department. Just polish up your boots and put on that black Stetson I've seen you wear when you go out sometimes. Believe me, heads will turn enough."

I give Renee a call and end up leaving a message: "Gage and I are going to the benefit tonight. Hope you will join us." After a few minutes, she texts back.

Great idea! I'll see you there, 6 p.m.

CHAPTER 11

Crystal.

"It was a beautiful day out on the water. Thank you. I am enjoying my time with you very much."

I smile at Henry; his face seems soft and sincere. I notice the tan lines around his eyes and nose from wearing sunglasses. He was very pale before he came for his visit. "I'm glad you enjoyed it. I am enjoying being with you, too. By the way, when you look in the mirror later, you might notice you resemble a raccoon."

He drops the car visor down to check his face then laughs. "I thought I put on enough sunblock. You'd never know I live in California and travel to the French Riviera all the time, right? I just always seem to be so busy that I rarely get much time out in the sun."

"Florida sun is strong anyway, but being on the water reflects even more. Hopefully it won't hurt. I plan on kissing that face all night."

He eyes me like a Great White then leans in for a kiss. He dives in deeper with his tongue as he tries to pull my body closer, but the center console of my car is in the way. I break from the lip lock. We are a little out of breath.

"Save a little for later, counselor," I murmur.

He raises an eyebrow, still looking sharkish. "There's something else I can't wait for you to put on my face." He makes a low growl.

I mirror his raised brow and match his smile. "I love the way you think."

He takes my hand, placing tender kisses on my wrist. "I love to watch you squirm, and I love all the sounds you make when you come for me."

My breath catches as my heart races and warmth rushes from my core to the rest of my body. "We have plenty of time before dinner reservations tonight. Let's get home!"

He starts the car, revving my little silver Mercedes SLC Roadster, and gets us safely home in record time.

Renee.

Slipping into my dark-denim skinny jeans and black, glittery top, I pace the closet to determine the best complement for my outfit: sandals, high heel stilettos, or boots. As I try to make up my mind, my cell buzzes. It's G.W.

"Hey," I answer.

"Hi there. What you got going on tonight?"

"I'm going to a benefit dinner with a friend. It's something we do every year. What's up with you?"

"Well, I have another hour of work, then maybe I'll find some local bar with some of the guys, grab dinner, have a couple beers. I'll be on this site till Thursday. I'm looking forward to seeing you Friday night."

"Me, too. Have a good work week," I tell him.

"Thanks. I just wanted to check in with you, see how you're doing."

"I'm good. I'm having a good weekend, I suppose. And thank you for checking in. It's sweet of you."

"I just want to be a good buddy to ya."

"I can use a good buddy," I say with a smile.

"Okay, then. Go get yourself all pretty and have a good time."

"Thanks, G. You have a good night yourself."

I put down my cell and think aloud, "High heels!"

I finish my look with some of my jewelry—diamond earrings, one of my simple diamond necklaces, and a couple of very sparkly tennis bracelets. With a smile, I remember my eighteenth birthday, when my mother gave me my first tennis bracelet. I also remember when Frank bought me so many of my diamond pieces for Christmases and anniversaries. It feels almost wrong to wear them, and those memories make me gloomy, a little misplaced in my soul.

More of a reason to go out tonight and have fun, I assure myself.

I am excited that Dusty will be bringing Gage, and I'm looking forward to getting to know him. They are certainly going to turn heads tonight. I can't wait to see what the snobs will gossip about tomorrow.

I drive up to the valet station at our local club, Halifax Beach and Golf Resort. As I hand over the keys to my Escalade, I hear my cell buzz and glance to see a text from Dusty.

Pulling up now in Gage's truck.

I look up from my phone and scan the parking lot, then I see them pulling up right in front of the station in an older-model Chevy Silverado dually. It wasn't falling apart, but anyone could see this truck has been around for a while. When Dusty and Gage get out, the truck's doors sound like they could use some oil, and when Gage hands the key to the valet, the poor kid looks like he wants to be anywhere but there, driving that. The young guys who work here are used to fancy sports cars and expensive SUVs. I work hard to try not to let my huge grin at this turn into a full-blown laugh.

Dusty has the same smile on her face as she walks over and gives me a hello hug. She and Gage look amazing together, and anyone can see the look of new love in their eyes. Dusty wears a similar ensemble to mine, but I notice she has on a black cowboy hat with a glittering rhinestone band around the crown.

"You look amazing! I'm loving the hat."

"Thanks, girlfriend. I'm loving the hat, too. Gage picked it up for me earlier."

I turn to get a better look at Gage. He is already in motion with his hand out to shake mine. "Hello, Miss Renee. Nice to see you again. It will be good to sit, talk, and get to know you better, instead of just a wave across the yard while I'm working at the ranch."

"Yes—you, too, Gage. Nice to see you here. I'm so happy you and Dusty found each other."

"Thank you, Renee. Dusty does something special to my heart, that's for sure. Now, shall I escort you ladies inside?"

Dusty and I each take an offered arm from Gage and enter the lobby. Our presence is acknowledged immediately. As heads turn in our direction, we can hear the whispers buzzing.

"Wow, we're a hit!" I say sarcastically.

"Yep, you hear that?" Dusty mumbles. "It's the sound of shock, jealousy, and ignorance, and it's music to my ears."

I let out a little laugh and toss a glance around the room. I spy a few of the usual crowd and wave or say hello here and there. I hear Dusty say to Gage, "Don't be nervous."

Gage flashes his brilliant, white gleam at her. "Nervous about what?" he says, giving her a peck on the cheek.

We find our table, and Gage asks what we would like to drink. Dusty and I look first at each other and then at him. "Of course," he says with a chuckle. "How could I forget? You want red or white?"

"I'm in the mood for a cabernet tonight."

"Sounds good. I second that," Dusty replies.

As Gage leaves to get our beverages, Dusty motions with her eyes. I squint through the crowd, and here comes Frank. "Hi, girls," he says with a sad smile, and I feel a little bad for him. "Renee, you look stunning. You too, Dusty."

"Thanks. Frank, what are you doing here?"

"Renee, you and I have always come to this benefit. I thought I should come and support the charity, anyway. I really had no idea you would be here, too, but I'm glad you are. Look, I don't want to get into it here, but I miss you terribly."

"I know you do, Frank. I'm sorry. Are you sitting at this table?"

"Well, it is our regular table. I didn't know it would be Dusty's tonight, as well. But we can have a nice night and sit and have dinner at the same table, can't we?"

"Yes...yes, we can. Just don't...let's not talk about things tonight. I just want to have fun."

"I agree—especially the fun part."

"Okay. Great," I utter.

"Here you go, ladies. Two cabernets."

Dusty and I take our glasses from Gage and take big gulps. "Thank you, Gage," I say.

"Uh, Gage, is it? I can get my wife her drinks for the rest of the evening. Thank you."

"Frank!" His name comes out of me in a low growl between my teeth. Gage reaches his hand out to Frank to shake it while he introduces himself as Dusty's date.

"Oh, sorry. I, uh, didn't know who..."

"I came alone and met them here, Frank. I don't have a date," I added.

"Right. Okay. Sorry about the confusion. Nice to meet you, Gage."

"Really, Frank. What happened to the nice time and just having fun?"

"You're right. I'm sorry."

Dusty and I pull out our chairs and sit next to each other, Gage on her left, Frank on my right. Dusty eyes Frank, and when he's not paying attention to us, she silently mouths the words *Oh my God* to me.

"Did you know he'd be here?" I ask her in a loud whisper, not caring if he heard or not.

"No! I swear—not a clue," she says, holding up her right hand.

I give her a pointed eyebrow and pursed lips.

"What? You don't believe me?" she says with a little grin to her mouth.

I squint my eyes at her.

"Okay. Shit, I knew he might be here, but I swear I didn't talk to him about...much..."

"Yeah...not much. Thanks."

"Okay, don't be mad. It wasn't like a thing I created. The benefit letters go to his email. I didn't think he'd come this year, especially without you, and he didn't think you would either. Just relax and have fun."

"Fine. Whatever," I say, a tiny bit annoyed, and take another big sip of my wine.

* * *

Dusty.

167

"You okay, darlin'?"

"Yes, Gage. I'm fine. Why do you keep asking?"

"Well, you have a lot going on. We got these uppity folks checkin' me out, and I don't want you to feel uncomfortable about it. Second, I am assuming you might have been the mastermind behind getting Renee and her husband together for the evening. If you are or not—and I don't care—I just want you to have a good time, because if you aren't, I'll take you home."

I smile at Gage, stand up, and hold out my hand. "Let's dance, cowboy. I love this song."

He listens for a second, recognizing the Brett Young tune, "In Case You Didn't Know," then returns my smile as he takes both my hands and leads me to the dance floor. I pull him in close, and he holds me so tightly we don't care about anything or anyone. Just us in this moment.

The song finishes, and I see Renee walking out to the lobby. Gage leans down to kiss me, "Go check on her, darlin'. I'll hang out here and get to know Frank."

"Thanks, Gage. You'll like him. He loves her madly. We all believe she's going through a postpartum depression. I didn't really set this up, but let's just say I did give it a little push."

"And that doesn't surprise me one bit," he says. "Go on." He waves his hand at me.

"Thank you. I'll be right back."

I race out to follow Renee and spot her walking to the pathway that leads to the golf course. "Renee, wait up!"

She stops. "I just need some air."

I walk out with her, and she finds a bench and plops herself down hard.

"What's the matter? Did Frank piss you off?"

"No, I think I'm pissing myself off. I saw you guys dancing, saw the love you both have in your eyes. I want that...I want to feel that again."

I sit down next to her, but I don't say anything. At this point, with what she's feeling, there is nothing I can say. All I can do is be here and listen.

"I want to feel that kind of love. I want someone to look at me the way Gage looks at you. I want butterflies and sweaty palms. I want romance. I want a pet name like *darlin'*, or *baby*, and I want to have crazy sex in weird places!"

As she says that, two older women walk by, stop, and stare at us.

I calmly turn in their direction. "Oh, please. Like you never."

The two older ladies quickly decide to keep moving, but I keep my eye on them as they approach the doors. As one turns her glance back to us, she gives us a small smile and a wink.

I look at Renee and we burst into belly-crunching laughter.

After a moment, we calm down enough to speak. "Renee, listen: I really do understand what you're saying. But when I see Frank look at you, and I see the years you have put in and the two beautiful baby girls you have, well, I get a little jealous of that. You need to count your blessings. Whatever you're going through, I just know it's going to pass."

"I hope so. I feel like every couple of weeks, my moods change about everything. G.W called me earlier, and as much as it made me happy to hear from him, I really didn't care. He works out of the area so much, he wouldn't really be around for me. I don't want that either."

"Aren't you seeing him again?"

"Yes, on Friday. It's a whole week away. I could cancel it, but I'm so confused."

"Look, don't do anything. You have time. You don't have to decide anything yet. On Monday, let's call Crystal and see if we can have a girls' night sometime during the week. She'll be dying to tell us about her weekend with Henry. I think you'll do better with a girl pow wow."

As I finish my sentence, I hear the doors open again and see Frank and Gage heading toward us.

"What's wrong?" I ask.

"Nothing," Frank says. "I wanted to come out and see if Renee was okay."

I nudge my girlfriend's arm. "See—he cares."

Renee stands and fixes her sparkly shirt. "I just needed some air; it got a little hot in there."

"Yeah, just some girl talk," I add.

The four of us stroll back in as Gage takes my arm and wraps it around his. We walk at a slower pace and let Frank and Renee get ahead of us. "They're serving dinner now, so I wanted to come and find you both. Frank wanted to tag along. He's heartbroken. He told me he follows her and tracks her moves.

He worries about her. He knows she's been dating, and he doesn't like it."

I stop and turn to Gage. "Following her? Like, in his car, following her around town?"

"Yes, that's how it sounds to me."

"Jesus, what do I do with that information?"

Gage shrugs. "Nothing. If you tell her, she will just get even more angry with him, and he will continue to do it anyway. You told me Renee is going through a depression because of hormones? I get it. You think she's going to come around, and yeah, she might, so don't add any more logs to this fire. Just let it ride."

"Agreed." I nod. "Now, let's eat. I'm starved."

CHAPTER 12

Crystal.

I arrive at Renee's house for our girls' night on time for once.

Dusty is just stepping out of her car, too. "Hey, I want to hear all about your weekend with Henry!"

"I'm sure! I definitely have happy, sexy things to tell," she says with a wink.

As we approach the front door, Renee opens it before we can ring the bell. "Come on—get in here!"

She hurries back to her kitchen, where she has already poured the wine and set out the usual snacks.

"Spill it," Renee demands. "How was the weekend with Henry?"

"Amazing." I look at them both, raise my eyebrows, and smile from ear to ear. "He is simply amazing. We have the same tastes, like the same music, have the same mindset. We are both attorneys. I mean, seriously, how much more in common could we have? It's just a shame he lives so far away. Long-distance relationships...I don't know. Can they work?"

"I think you should give it a try. You are positively glowing!" Dusty exclaims.

"Undeniable," Renee adds. "You are glowing. You seem different, too. Calmer...more relaxed, maybe?"

I nod in agreement. "It's true. Henry, I believe, may be the one." The girls gasp and smile. "Even making love is really special with him."

"Making love?" Renee coos. "That is the last word I thought I'd ever hear from your mouth. Wow! Someone is melting the ice princess. I can't wait to meet this Romeo."

"We went out on the boat and to the Hard Rock Casino over in Hollywood. He's a great dancer. And a great lover."

"Give us some dirt. Come on—out with it," Dusty says with a laugh.

"Well, he's gentle but strong. His kisses take my breath away. And he loves to take care of me first. I've never had a lover so tuned into details." The girls lean in closer, looking like hungry wolves.

"Go on. WE need details," Renee encourages.

"Well, he just seems to know where all my triggers are. He uses everything on me. Absolutely drives me crazy and gets me soaking wet. His fingers, his tongue...and oh my God! The cock on this man! He just pulled me on top of him, slid me right down on it— and believe me, he was rock-hard and huge— and I rode it till I came so hard that I actually screamed. No moans and groans, ladies—I screamed. Then, he lifted me off him and tossed me onto his face. Just...mmmm...worked me out again with that mouth of his till I fell over in a quivering heap. That's when he got on top and took me again. I had three orgasms...THREE!"

"Jesus!" Dusty exclaims. She and Renee were both squirming in their seats.

"That's hot," Renee says as she takes a big gulp of her wine.

"Yes, girls, I get horny even thinking about it. I can't let a man like that escape."

"No, no!" they say in unison.

Dusty takes a good sip of wine. "Well, Gage doesn't know it yet, but he is in for some experimentation tonight."

"Oh great. And I don't have anyone to go home to," Renee scoffs.

"Sure you do," I tell her. "You have BOB."

"She lifts her glass. "So I do! Cheers!" We laugh.

"How are you and Gage getting along?" I ask, and Dusty looks at me with the same dopey smile I'm wearing.

"We are doing great. He came with Renee and me to the *Denim and Diamonds* benefit."

"Oh, I'm sure you are all the talk of the town, now!" I laugh.

"Yes, we definitely turned some heads and heard the whispers. But you know what? I don't care. Gage has more integrity and class than most of the bozos at the club. None of it bothered him, either. The whole night he was just concerned for my well-being, and we danced, we ate, we had fun. The more we showed everyone we were together and happy, the more I really didn't hear the whispers anymore. When we got home, we made love, and he was so tender and sweet."

"Good for you! I'm truly happy for you, Dusty. You deserve a good man in your life. We all do. What about you, Renee? You bored with dating? You going to give Frank a chance?"

"Frank was at the benefit, and Crazyhorse over here was behind it." Renee points to Dusty. "I was flooded with all kinds of mixed emotions being there with him. In some ways, I feel bad for him, and I love him, but I can't stand him—all at the same time!" she says with a little cry in her voice.

"Hey, I wasn't totally responsible for him attending. I told you the emails go out to everyone who is a club member." Dusty states it as a fact.

I laugh at her remark, and she eyes me. "Oh, you sound like a lawyer. Quit defending yourself. Didn't you think to block it from going to him?" I ask her.

"OKAY...I thought by the time the benefit came around, maybe something would spark for them...well, her. He is still devastated."

"Spark? The only spark I felt was anger," Renee says softly.

We just sit there for a moment, drinking wine, munching on pretzels, and letting Renee have a small sob. "I have a date tomorrow night. Should I cancel it?"

"Who's it with?" I ask.

"G.W. He wants to go on a beach picnic over at Luna Park."

"Oh, I used to like to do that, but I thought your last date with this guy went a little strange?"

"It did, but we talked. He said he was nervous and didn't intend to be creepy. And I think it's cute—he calls me his little buddy."

Dusty wrinkles her nose. "Little buddy? You like that?"

"Kind of. I think it's sweet."

A thought of my ex pops into my head. "Greg would call me that sometimes. Men can be so stupid. Anyway, yes, I think you should cancel the date."

Dusty raises her hand. "I do, too."

"Really? Both of you think I should cancel? Why? Because you both found happiness and I can't?"

"Oh my God, Renee!" Dusty yells. "That's not what we're saying at all. I just think this is another flaky dude that you don't need to get aggravated over."

"Renee, the fact that you just said what you did should tell you how much you're not in the right frame of mind. Your hormones are confused; you're hyper-emotional. Dusty's right—he sounds like a flake." Dusty and I look at each other and then back at Renee. I can see her tensing up, fists balling at each side. "Don't get mad at us; we are trying to look out for you," I quickly add.

Renee takes a deep breath then exhales like a bull. "I understand, but this whole dating thing was your idea. Everyone's in, it was for fun, no one was supposed to fall in love, and now the both of you have found love. You both keep telling me not to get attached, and what did YOU do, both of you?"

"Okay, we found love, but not on the *Blind Date* site. You have to admit, we didn't know how horrible those men would be. None of us did. And neither I nor Dusty knew we were going to find love. Renee, you have love already. Frank loves you."

"Don't push her, Crystal," Dusty interjects then turns to Renee. "I love you. I'm here for you. Whatever you decide."

"Thank you. I'm feeling a bit tired. I'd like to go to bed, girls. I hate to cut the evening short, but I'm getting a headache."

I eye Dusty then observe Renee. I have so much more to say but decide to hold my tongue after a moment of contemplation. "All right, Renee. Get some sleep. We will talk in the morning."

"Fine. Thanks for understanding. Good night, girls," she says and heads upstairs, leaving Dusty and me to exit on our own. We silently wash the wine glasses, put some of the snacks away, and let ourselves out.

We end up just standing in Renee's driveway, scratching our heads.

"Wow," I say to Dusty. "That went downhill fast."

"Yep, I've been meaning to call you. She's going to need help if she doesn't snap out of this soon. You don't think she'll get worse or do something foolish, do you?"

"No, she just seems to be a little too sensitive, but I think we should tell Frank how tonight went."

"Oh yeah—about that. Frank told Gage that he too has been very concerned for Renee. He apparently follows her and tracks her moves, so he knows where she is, knows she's been on dates. I didn't tell her. Even Gage doesn't think we should say anything that might make her more upset or angry. And, well, after what just happened with us tonight, I'm glad Frank is following her."

"Yeah, let's keep that under our hats for now. Be careful driving home. Talk you tomorrow."

Dusty gets in her car and shouts, "Good night, Crystal!" from the window. I wave back as I climb into my Mercedes. My mind races and wanders. I feel bad. This stupid dating thing was my idea, but I sure didn't mean for it to hurt Renee, although I think there are other factors at play here, too. But regardless, I feel sad for my sweet friend.

* * *

Renee.

I'm lying here in bed, wide awake. I'm so angry, but why? I feel hurt, but by whom? Why am I confused?

0I p0ress the T.V. remote, and the nightly news bursts into a story about another rape victim from Oakland Park. This time the news is better: she survived the attack but is in critical condition. This is frightening. I feel the need to talk to someone, and I call G.W.

"Hello."

"Hey, G.W.? It's Renee."

"Yeah, I know. What...uh, what ya doing up so late?"

"Is it okay that I called? Did I wake you? I'm sorry."

"Yep. Nope, I was out, but it's all right. Are you okay?"

"I'm fine. Just couldn't sleep. Never mind. It's nothing."

"No, no. You got me on the phone, now, so go on—spill it. What's on your mind?"

"I was with my friends this evening, and I'm just a tad bit angry with them. So I just wanted to talk to someone other than them."

"What'd they say that got you up and about?"

"It's kind of stupid but going on the dating site was supposed to be for fun, and now they've both found love, and it wasn't supposed to be this way. They keep telling me not to get attached, but they ended up attached and happy. Okay, not with someone they met online, but still. And now that I say this aloud, it really sounds childish."

"No, I get it. Kind of makes you feel a little left out of their world."

"Yes! That's exactly how I feel. I don't ever want to be jealous of my friends. I am happy for them—envious, but happy."

"They probably told you to quit the site, too, maybe even break off tomorrow night's date with me?"

"Yep, G.W., they actually did. Both of them keep pushing me to go back to my husband. I don't know why they won't listen to me or understand what I feel."

"Sounds to me like they are just concerned for you; it's what friends generally do. Do you want to cancel our date tomorrow evening?"

I am silent for a moment, hesitating to answer. I hear him exhale.

"Look, I'll understand. Maybe you are just not ready for all this, yet."

Now I feel bad. G.W. has always been nice to me. "No. No, I want to see you. You have always been easy to talk to except during that one weird, awkward lunch date."

He laughs. "Yeah, I agree. My nerves got the best of me that day. I apologize again."

"No worries. I'll see you over at the park tomorrow night."

"Yes, and give me a jingle if you need to, buddy."

I put my phone on the charger, turn off the T.V., and get comfortable under my blanket. Hopefully, a good night's rest will make a positive difference in the morning.

* * *

Dusty.

"Why you so quiet this morning, baby?"

I look up at Gage. He's washing a plate in the kitchen sink but has his eyes focused on me.

"I guess I am being pretty quiet. I don't like how I left Renee last night, and it compromised my sleep."

He steps over to the table where I'm sitting like a zombie. "Call her. I bet she'll talk it out with you." He bends to give me a kiss on top of my head. "You have a good day. I love you. And call your friend."

I smile as best I can and watch Gage leave through the back door to tend to the ranch. I know it's early in this relationship, and I feel very lucky. I suppose Crystal does, too. I can see how Renee would feel left out, but her emotions seem magnified and erratic right now. I take a big gulp of my coffee and hit Renee's number on my cell.

"Hi." Renee's voice sounds small.

"Hey, are you feeling better this morning? Because I'm not. Neither Crystal nor I want you to be upset."

"No, I know. I'm just feeling vulnerable a lot lately. Both of you have it all going on. A business, high-powered career, horses, and now great guys. I feel like I can't compete. I feel like a loser. And yes, I get mad at you both for not understanding my feelings. Maybe I'm more emotional than you guys, but my separation is still very recent, and I've

got two little ones, too. I don't have a job. I
don't have anything else in my life except
being someone's mom, wife...I do for
everyone. I want some fun. I want to be
loved."

"Renee, you are loved. You're just, I don't
know, blocked or something. We just want
you to understand we care about you and
think you might be having some type of
depression brought on by all the hormonal
changes. We're certainly not doctors like
Frank is, but I remember you told me two
weeks after you gave birth that you didn't
want Frank to touch you, you just couldn't
stand him. Look, all I'm saying is that's not
normal, but it is normal behavior for
postpartum depression."

"There it is again."

"What?"

"You and Crystal—you boss me around
like I'm a baby. The lectures you both hand
out to me are insulting. Why won't you both
take the time to understand how much I'm
hurting inside and stop putting a label on it?"

"Renee, we have! You're not acting like
yourself. All we want is for you to talk with
your doctor about the possibility of the
hormonal changes coloring the way you are
feeling. Please—I don't want to argue. I am

185

your friend, and I never want to hurt you. I'm here for you. So I'm changing the subject. Are you going on your date tonight?"

"Yes, I talked to him last night. He was very understanding about my feelings. I think he's going to be a nice guy after all. I like how he says, 'Give me a jingle,' and he called me buddy again. It's different. Makes me feel good somehow."

I bite my tongue and take a deep breath. "Okay, just take your phone and your mace, and I'll be your backup tonight if you need me."

"Thanks. I'll let you know how it goes."

I hang up, take my mug of coffee outside, and sit in my rocker. Gage is over by the stalls and spots me from across the horse arena. I give him a thumb's up, and he returns one back. Even though I'm not pleased with my and Renee's conversation, it could have been worse.

CHAPTER 13

Renee.

I spent a good part of my day getting a manicure and pedicure done for tonight, and now I'm glancing through my closet to find something comfortable to wear. I end up choosing light cotton jeans and a multi-colored, loose-fitting, peasant-style shirt that sweetly hangs off one of my tanned shoulders. I put my hair neatly in a ponytail, apply light makeup, and complement my look with big silver hoop earrings. Lastly, I slip on my white-and-silver sandals, and I'm ready to go meet G.W.

I see Crystal has tried to contact me, but I'll call her tomorrow. I'm in too good of a mood right now. I grab my purse and a bottle of wine to bring on the picnic date, and I realize I'm feeling better about meeting G.W. I'm thinking it's going to be a good date.

* * *

Crystal.

"I really had a great time with you. I miss you, darling."

"I miss you, too, Henry. I'm already planning a trip to France to see you and visit my mother. I talked with her after you left. She is pleased with herself about her good matchmaking skills."

"I'll bet she is. I have not seen her or my mother, yet, since I've been back. I have no doubt they are talking us up to their little social community."

"Yes, I agree. I will let you know ASAP when I'm coming. My schedule right now is all over the place, but it won't stay that way for long."

"Sounds good. I'll call you later, darling."

"I'll be waiting."

The smile that covers my face is indisputable. Henry is something special.

A knock at my door snaps me back to reality. I glance up to see Meredith standing there. "Your friend Dusty is here."

"Really? Let her in."

Within a few seconds, Dusty is standing at my desk. She looks disturbed. "Please tell me you have wine in that fridge over there."

"Yes."

"It's way past five, and it's Friday night."

"Correct again," I say with a smile.

"So why am I drinking with you at your office?"

"Is this a trick question or a loaded one?" I ask her.

She sits on my sofa and makes herself comfortable. "Well, I texted you and asked when you were leaving work, because I needed to talk, remember? You said you weren't sure. I texted a little while ago at six, and you said you were still here, so here I am."

I got up, kicked my shoes off, and sat with her. "Something's really bothering you. Go ahead. I'm done. I was going to come in for a little while tomorrow, anyway."

"Have you talked with Renee?"

"Nope, I called her twice today and it went to voicemail. I suppose she's really pissed off. I am hoping in a day or two we can all get together and talk. I feel bad about what happened last night, but you know how she's been lately. She'll come around."

"I talked to her this morning. She's not happy with us at all. She thinks we treat her like a baby and that we are not really listening to her. She told me she feels like she's nothing; she wants more."

I raise my eyebrows. "Well, she's been very emotional. Anything we say to her either ends with her in tears or getting angry. We know what the deal is."

"We do. She does not."

"What do you think we should do?"

"That's why I'm here, Crystal, drinking wine with you in your office. Let's figure out a solution without losing our friend."

"Fine. Do we sit her down and have an intervention? Because, Dusty, I have to tell you, I don't think that's the way to go."

"I was thinking of something with Frank, but right now when she looks at him, she cringes. It's so sad; my heart breaks."

"They got along at the benefit, though, right?"

"Well, yeah...barely."

"Did she go on that date?"

"Yes, she should be with him now." Dusty checks her watch. "She talked to him last night sometime after we left. Said he made her feel better and he was being very sweet.

Called her his 'buddy' again. She said it's cute the way he says, 'Give me a jingle.'"

I take a sip of my wine. I'm just about to say something when I suddenly get a flash of recognition. "Wait a minute. He says buddy AND jingle? That's what Greg used to say..."

"Oh, you don't think..." Dusty looks at me with big eyes.

"G.W. Greg Walker...Oh God, don't tell me she's on a date with my ex-husband, Greg fucking Walker!"

"Okay, calm down. It could be a coincidence. When was the last time you've even seen him? I thought he moved away."

"He did, but it's been years. That weasel could have come back. Who knows with him." I grab my cell and call Renee, "Pick up! Pick up! Shit—voicemail. Where are they going?"

"What are you going to do, just crash the date? Spy on them?" Dusty asks

"I'm going to make sure it's not him, because if it is, YES I'm going to drag her out of there, away from that loser. She's so vulnerable right now, that asshole will charm the pants right off her, and he probably has herpes, or worse! Please tell me you know where they went."

"Oh...hmm..." Snapping my fingers, I wrack my brain. "LUNAR PARK!" I blurt out. "Let's go!"

***

Renee.

I pull into the parking lot of Lunar Park. G.W. is here already and leaning against a cream-colored van. I pull up next to him and get out of my vehicle. "Hey, is this your work van?"

"Yep, basically. Come on—I found a good spot and laid out a blanket for our picnic."

I follow along the path, and soon I hear and smell the ocean. G.W. points to a secluded area with just a little break in the trees to allow us to have a view of the beach. I show him the bottle of wine I brought, and he points to one already chilling in a little plastic bucket.

"I'll open that one since I have it on ice. Sit. Get yourself cozy."

I do as he says. "This is really nice, G.W. Really. Such a great idea. It's a beautiful night. Do you have a lantern? It's getting dark."

"I do," he says and lights it up.

I inspect the blanket and notice a lovely picnic spread with cheeses, crackers, and fruit. "Wow, you've got a nice little feast going on for us."

"Thank you. I try. I wasn't sure what you would like, so I grabbed some of this and that. My hope is that we can get to know each other better and drop all the bullshit."

I laugh a little but quickly realize he isn't joking. His face is serious. He reaches over to the bottle of wine, opens it, pours two cups, and hands me one. I take the cup and smell the oaky chardonnay wafting up to my nose. "Thank you, and what bullshit are you talking about?"

"Oh, you know. The kind where you haven't told me your last name and all, or maybe how many dates you've been on since you went on the *Blind Date* website."

He's getting weird again. "Well, how about you tell me your name? What does G.W. stand for?"

"Greg William. Now your turn. Tell me about yourself, your last name, your kids' names."

"Well, okay. My last name is Valano. I have two little girls, Samantha and Amanda. Sami's the baby."

"Go on. What does your husband do?"

"No, your turn again. Where are you from?"

"The South," he says with a small smile. He is staring at me so intently, I don't know if it's endearing or creepy.

"Now look who's handing out bull. The South—really?" I say, laughing.

He hands me a small plate with various fruits and cheeses. Quietly, we sit and eat while watching the few strangers who jog or bike-ride by along the path in the distance. The sun has set, and the beach-lovers who had set up camp that day have all left.

"Doesn't the park close when it's dark?"

He smiles. "Yes, but that's the beauty. No one is here, and I gotcha all to myself." He leans in for a kiss, and I submit to it, but I'm feeling bad vibes. I break the kiss and act like I'm cleaning up our picnic mess. "Won't our cars get fines? We should go somewhere." In my head I'm thinking, *Somewhere very public.*

He tugs my arm and forcefully pulls me over to him. The movement throws me off my knees, and suddenly I'm on my back. He scrambles on top of me, and I can barely move. With one hand, he secures both my wrists while his other hand is groping my body. Up under my shirt, he roughly squeezes my breast, and it's not pleasant. "G.W., STOP!"

His mouth is by my ear. "You know you want it," he growls. "Now, be a good buddy and let me have your pussy and you won't get your pretty little head bashed in so bad. I let that other slut live. I could have killed her, too, but I only killed the ones that fought me. They deserved it."

I let out a scream, and he smacks me so hard I get dizzy. I try to get away, try to focus. I can't believe this is happening. Anger starts to boil in my veins. I think of my babies. With all my might, I buck like a mad bull and it throws him off of me. I try to crawl to my purse, but he tugs at my calves. I kick with everything I've got so I can get to it. Blindly, I find the mace and let him have it. He is screaming, and with every profane name he calls me, my rage grows even more into a burning fury. I reach for the wine bottle I brought, and with every ounce of strength in my crazed wrath, I scream and slam that bottle into the side of his head. He drops like a bowling ball.

I'm shaking, and my heart is pounding so hard I feel as though it might burst.

"Renee!" I hear my name and turn to see Frank running up to me.

"FRANK!"

"Oh my God, Renee! Are you all right?"

I drop to my knees, trying to catch my breath enough to speak. "Oh shit, Frank...He's the rapist. He...he tried to..."

Vomit spurts from my stomach like a fountain. Frank steps over to me and holds me, telling me stuff like the doctor that he is. "You're fine, now. It's okay. Just breathe," he says in a calming voice. He grabs the blanket and drapes it over me, wanting me to sit down, but I can't. He goes over to G.W. to assess the damage. "He's dead, Renee. You got him squarely on the temple."

"RENEE!" I hear my name again and squint through the darkness to see two figures with flashlights.

Frank stands up from G.W.'s lifeless body. "It's Crystal and Dusty," he tells me.

As they come upon the scene, Dusty puts her hand over her mouth then steps over to me to hold me. Crystal steps over to G.W. "Oh my God! It is Greg! Renee, you went on a date with my ex-husband, Greg Walker! What happened? What's wrong with him?"

I manage with my next breath to choke out, "He...he's the rapist. He was gonna...and he confessed, and I..."

"Shhhh," Dusty says. "It's over. Frank, you knocked him out good."

"No, Renee did. She killed him, Crystal. He's dead."

Without warning, in one slick motion, Crystal pulls out her gun and puts two bullets in him. The sound and action jolt us, making us yell and crouch to the ground.

"I killed him! What are you doing?" I whimper.

Crystal steps back, locks her gun, and places it back in her purse. "I'm making sure that son of bitch stays dead."

"What the fuck?" Dusty snaps. "Renee killed him, Crystal. She wouldn't have gotten in trouble for self-defense, but how do we explain the gunshot wounds? Do we say we all were witnesses?"

"No," Crystal abruptly says. "I can't be involved in anything; I could get disbarred. None of us really should be involved. You all know this city and its politics."

"Yes, but we might get praised," Dusty adds.

"As a lawyer, let me break this down for all of you. We have all been accessories to a murder. It must be proven what killed him, the blow to the head or the gunshots. If it's the head wound, it's Renee's word against the court that he is the rapist. Not to mention I will get charged with desecration of a body. Frank, you're a doctor. You're at the scene. You will probably get suspended from the hospital, or worse. We will sit in jail for a few days, maybe a week, and then the court hearing and everything that goes along with it may go on for months, possibly a year or two. Proving he's responsible for the rapes with DNA is a process. To make matters worse, even if we are found innocent, this will be on the news, in the media, our faces will be everywhere, and who the hell knows who else Greg Walker is involved with that might surface and make more trouble, like his mother, and I'm sure she would love to see me rot in hell. Are you ready for all that? Because I gotta tell ya, I'm not in the mood for it, especially over this piece of shit!"

"I'm definitely not in the mood," I whisper.

Dusty rubs her forehead. "Okay, so what now? We get rid of the body and call it day?"

"Sounds good to me," Frank states.

Within minutes, a plan is born. We all look at each other and nod in agreement. Moving fast, we clean up the area. We roll up Greg's body in the blanket, and Frank and Crystal haul it back to the parking lot after we make sure all is clear.

With little effort, we find the keys to the van. When we get it open, we see the usual tools lying about, but the one that gives us chills is the bloody sledgehammer. The crazy bastard didn't even clean it. We are careful not to touch it as we slip Greg's body into the van. Frank gets in the driver's seat and suggests we take the back roads down to the docks. He will meet us there.

CHAPTER 14

Renee.

We park on the landing. It is a very calm night, and thankfully very few people are hanging out, drinking on their boats. We are quiet as we pad our way down the wooden dock to Crystal's boat and climb aboard. She starts it up and maneuvers over to the launch area. Then we wait what seems an eternity for Frank to show up. When he finally arrives, Crystal backs up the boat good and close, and we all help Frank on board, along with Greg's body. It is heavier than before. Frank has tied the bloody sledgehammer and various weights onto him to ensure he sinks.

"Ready?" Crystal eyes each of us. We nod. She sits in her captain's chair and hauls ass out into the Atlantic Ocean.

"I'm going to get us at least two hours out. That should do it."

Dusty sends a text to Gage, telling him she is with us and she will be home later than normal. "I can't tell Gage about any of this.

There are already too many of us involved. God forbid something goes wrong, I won't let him be another accomplice. If I ever do tell him, it will be after we are married thirty years, and then when I'm eighty, I might mention it."

We chuckle with nervous laughter while I am still feeling very sick to my stomach. I look over at Frank. He shuffles over to me and encircles me with his protective, reassuring arms.

"How are you holding up?" he whispers.

In that moment, something clicks, a reawakening of sorts. I see Frank with the love I used to have in my eyes. I see him—really see him. The pent-up anger melts, and the release is overwhelming. Tears sting my eyes, and I grab at Frank and hold him as if I had been lost and now found.

"I'm so sorry! What have I done?" I cry out. "I'm so sorry! I love you, Frank. I do! Can you forgive me?"

"Shhh...my girl. Yes, it's fine. It's all right," he whispers.

"It's the trauma," he says to us. "It could be what snapped her back."

"Thank God!" Crystal shouts.

Dusty smiles and places her hand over her mouth then drops it and says, "Welcome back. You're gonna be okay; we are all going to be okay...I hope."

For an hour and forty-five minutes, I sit snugly in Frank's embrace, going in and out of crying spells. After a night like this, I will never doubt the love my husband has for me. He is such a good man.

Finally, around midnight, we toss Greg's body off the boat and watch it sink. It's eerily quiet and calm, but the full moon is so bright we don't need flashlights to see around the boat. Its glow glitters off the water like it is guiding us back toward home. No words are spoken during the two-hour trip back. Crystal docks the boat and Frank breaks the silence by telling us he knows where he can ditch the van and leave it. A bad side of town. It will get stripped and probably set on fire.

The whole weekend goes by without any communication from Crystal or Dusty. Frank and I enjoy rediscovering each other and our relationship and talking things out. I can see things more clearly now, even though I realize a hormonal imbalance cannot really disappear overnight. But I had not recognized that it had been putting me in sort of a fog that distorted my perception. In a way, I had been harming myself, Frank, and our children. It was like I was another person. I promise Frank I will now talk to my doctor and take medication if I still need it. I do understand now why I've not been well. But I also know I am loved and cherished by a husband who refused to give up on me, and on this Monday morning, I'm feeling very blessed.

* * *

Dusty.

For a whole week, I've kept myself busy. I watch the news every night, and...nothing. Not even a missing person. The woman who survived her attack can't remember anything but a scratchy voice with a Southern accent, which here in Florida does not narrow any margins.

My cell phone buzzes with a group text from Frank.

We have fire.

I shake my head but can't help the smile that forms on my face.

I send back a response.

BBQ at my house tomorrow night.

CHAPTER 15

Dusty's Barbecue.

"Gage, get the door, please. I heard the bell. I'm in the middle of chopping vegetables."

"Yes, darlin'. Sounding like the wife already."

I smile and glance up from my cutting board to see Crystal is the first to arrive. She comes right up to me and we hug as though we hadn't seen each other in months.

"How are you?" she asks in a low voice.

"I'm good, really. Although, what does that say about me?"

She grabs the bottle of wine I have open and pours herself a full glass. "It says we got rid of a bad guy. The end."

"Have you been watching the news? I have seen nothing."

She nods. "I agree; not a word. Have you talked to Renee?"

"No, but she and Frank should be here soon." I watch as Gage goes out to the barbecue pit with the food and shuts the door behind him. "All I told him was Renee had a little breakthrough, she and Frank are working it out, and you and I were there for moral support."

"Well, it's technically not a lie. I'm glad that Henry wasn't here so I don't have to worry about saying anything to him."

I inhale a big breath then let it out.

Crystal touches my arm. "We're good. It's all good. We got rid of his phone, his van. Burned his wallet. There's no way they can trace him to us. I took down the profile on the dating site, but thankfully there is nothing on there that's suspicious. The only one of us that would ever get questioned might be me if he comes up missing. I'm his ex-wife. Luckily, it's been years, and I'm miles above Greg's class. So let's not even worry about it."

I take another deep breath. "Deal."

*　*　*

Renee and Frank arrive about ten minutes later, and I'm happy to admit they look extremely in love. "Where's Gage? Out cooking by the pit?" Franks asks.

I nod. Frank tosses us a crooked smile. "I'll...uh...leave you girls alone a minute and keep Gage company." We wait as he exits through the French doors leading out to the patio.

"How are you holding up, Renee?" I ask her.

"I'm fine when I'm awake, but when I fall asleep, I have nightmares of Greg trying to rape me. When I wake from it, though, Frank is there, holding me, thank goodness. But I've got to tell you guys, I don't have any guilt about it nor does Frank. It doesn't matter who killed this man. We know the God's honest truth: I had to protect myself. I had no choice.

"Me either—no guilt here," I agree.

"That makes three of us." Crystal raises her wine glass.

Renee eyes each of us. "Neither one of you can tell your significant others what happened or what we did. Well, at least not for almost a lifetime. How will you deal with that?"

"I'm not taking the chance at all," I tell them. "For a week, I kept repeating in my head what we did, and I kept wondering when I was supposed to feel bad or guilty. As far as I'm concerned, we rid Fort Lauderdale, or the world, of a big piece of shit. But we don't need to be heroes in the spotlight for it. Not only was he hurting so many other women, he attacked one of our own. Renee, you fought back; you saved yourself; we were on our way to save you from him in a whole other shitty scenario. So we have to look at it, in a weird way, as a win-win."

"Exactly," Crystal retorts. "We don't feel guilty because we feel justified. That's what it makes us. Justified. So it's easier not to speak of it, hear of it, or see it as anything wrong. I was married to that asshole. I knew he wasn't right in the head, but I had no idea he was capable of killing someone! I feel more creeped out about that! But still, others would see US as a little fucked up in the head, too, if they knew what we had covered up. That's why we must forget it, be blind to it."

Renee picks up her wine glass. "Here's to us, three blind wives."

We clink our glasses, and somehow we manage a giggle, which grows into an all-out laughing-till-it-hurts episode. Maybe it's nervous energy; maybe it's relief. Whatever it is, we know we will be okay.

***

Renee.

After that night at Dusty's house, our lives seemed to go right back to normal. Weeks went by. Everyone was working at their careers. Everyone was falling in love and building relationships...or rebuilding, in our case.

Within a few months, Crystal went off to the south of France to visit her mother and spend time with Henry. In the time she was there, she discovered a new way of living, with less stress and an abundance of love. So she has decided to move to California, live with Henry, and work together with him, both in career and relationship. She leaves in two weeks.

Gage wanted Dusty to visit Montana and meet his family. They actually packed up the truck and drove cross-country. They had a great time, and Gage's family adores Dusty. He came into her life like a knight on a white horse. He handled her horses with respect and a deep communication, and you could say he did the same with her. He showed her such love and respect, breaking through her glass heart without shattering it and yet letting her soul remain wild. She loves him for who he is and who he lets her be, not for what he has or hasn't got.

I knew the minute Dusty set foot in the wide-open Big Sky State her soul would soar like an eagle. It is a place for her spirit, Gage, and the horses to run. She put the spa and Crooked Pines Ranch up for sale. Both are pending with buyers. In the meantime, Dusty and Gage have their hearts and eyes on a ranch out in Montana and want to work it together, enjoying a simple life. She also leaves for a while in two weeks.

As for me, I will miss them terribly. I have found a part-time job at a local magazine, writing articles about things happening in and around Fort Lauderdale. It's not about the money; Frank provides just fine. It's about me having a purpose besides being a wife and mother. My hormones seem to have gotten back in balance, and I am happy. I'm happy with Frank, our girls, my new job, and my life right here in Florida.

***

Driving away from the airport brings a spectrum of emotions. In some ways, it is heartbreaking. But I am also excited, looking forward to our future, visiting them, seeing their new places, possibly going to their weddings, and fulfilling our pact to meet somewhere for a fun girls' weekend on each of our birthdays. I watched each friend walk to two different terminals to board their planes, and though we are all on different paths now, I am at peace. Each of us has found our way to happiness.

And no one found out our secret.

The end.

January 9th, 2018

BAHAMA TRIBUNE.

Freeport police were called Thursday evening when human remains were discovered by beachgoers. Officers could not identify the remains, which appear to have washed onto the shore, and have turned them over to the coroner's office for further analysis. However, according to the police report, the remains are incomplete and have been severely compromised by the elements as well as various organisms. No identity or cause of death can yet be determined.

If you have any information regarding this case, please contact the Royal Bahamas Police Force in Freeport.

What can I say about this book? I can tell you this was my transition book. It took me a long time to write it even though I knew what I wanted to write. This story idea came to me right before my husband and I separated. So, I wanted to interview some single ladies, and I had some help from my married friends, too. Then, with really no shock, at forty-eight years old, I found myself going through a divorce and at the mercy of dating websites. I also can tell you that I cannot believe what really does go on. Every morning, I would go and read all the messages I had received. I would laugh about some of them all day, while others very much disturbed me to my core.

I still want to know why men you've never met would show you pictures of their junk and ask if you want it, all before going out on a date. I don't know—maybe I just have a lot of respect for myself—but I was not amused.

My advice is this: I don't really recommend it. However, if you do go on these dating sites, be careful and have a plan. Yes, I have heard great stories of people finding love, achieving a successful conclusion, but there are scary ones, too.

While on one particular dating site, I always felt as though I was walking on a tight rope without a net, and sadly, one time I did find myself in a bad situation. I was lucky enough to have friends nearby, which in fact helped me come up with Dusty's bar scene. That was a page out of my own personal files.

I suppose it's a good thing I didn't finish this story when I thought I would. As it turns out, I found myself involved in the very backdrop I had thought to write about and got an up-close and personal glance into a crazy experience!

Dedications

Thank you...

To Michael Ray King, author, writer, publisher. You never give up on me.

To all my wonderful friends who talk me off of ledges and make me laugh and tell me never to give up. Thank you for sharing stories, insight, and suggestions. All of it is so helpful in so many ways.

To Jorja Dupont-Oliva, my writing buddy. We bounce ideas off of each other, read each other's works in progress, motivate, inspire, cry, and laugh together.

To my love, Harry Oberbeck, who endearingly yells at me almost daily. In his words: "Get in your study and write, lady!"

To my editor, Karin Nicely, for your encouragement, for so graciously fine-tuning my words, and for helping me find my voice.

To all who buy my books and support me and leave reviews, THANK YOU! You make my day. You guys rock!

...And special thanks to my Angels. I know you're all around me. I know you give me signs in my dreams and in the light of day. I feel your strength when I can't find mine.

Dream* Wish * Believe.

As with all my books, music inspires my writing. Songs that motivated the writing of **_Three Blind Wives_**.

"The Shape of You" – Ed Sheeran

"Nobody Knows" – Pink

"Miss Independent" – Kelly Clarkson

"Only the Lonely" – The Motels

"In Case You Didn't Know" – Brett Young